SHURA   CHILDREN'S LIT.

The season of silence

DATE DUE			
3-6-84			

THE SEASON
OF SILENCE

———

THE SEASON OF SILENCE

Mary Francis Shura

ILLUSTRATED BY

Ruth Sanderson

762656

ATHENEUM 1976 NEW YORK

To Irene...
Who also remembers becoming.

Library of Congress Cataloging in Publication Data
Shura, Mary Francis. The season of silence.
SUMMARY: *The events following Susie's
long sickness in the spring changed her life
more than she ever imagined.*
I. Sanderson, Ruth II. Title.
PZ7.S55983Sc [Fic] 75-23194
ISBN 0-689-30513-3

Published simultaneously in Canada by
McClelland & Stewart, Ltd.
Manufactured in the United States of America by
H. Wolff, New York
Designed by Nora Sheehan
First Edition

Contents

The Changing Time

THE EASIEST THING in the world would have been for Susie Spinner to blame that whole strange spring on her strep throat. That would have been easy but not fair. Instead, Susie had a spooky certainty that the changes were hanging there in the darkness just beyond her knowing, waiting to happen. Her season of silence would have come, no matter what, she thought later.

But being sick and having to be shut away by herself all that time meant that she was to return, as if from a long journey, to find her life unexpectedly altered. It seemed as if some immense force had taken a firm hold on the layers of her life and twisted them so that what had been high became low and what had been firm and solid under her feet was suddenly spongy and terrifying.

She caught the strep throat late in March when everyone else seemed to have gotten over their winter things. At first her throat just hurt when she swallowed, then her cheeks felt as if they were on fire. Small round spots of bright red even appeared on them as if she had been slapped hard by invisible hands.

Her mother laid the back of her hand against Susie's throat right under her left ear as she always did, then gave a funny cry, almost like a yelp.

"This child is burning up with fever," she told Susie's father accusingly, as if he had personally set a match to his middle child.

Her father grinned at Susie and winked. "The fireman's name is Ramsey," he said. "Better give him a ring."

At first the trip to Dr. Ramsey was just as always. Susie waited outside with a horde of little children until her name was called. Then Dr. Ramsey thumped and listened and finally probed her throat with a cotton swab.

Then the difference began.

"Of course it could be only one of her regular sore throats," Dr. Ramsey said, with a tiny smile at Susie. "One of those she gets from puddle-walking or biking without a jacket or fooling around that old dank canal. But on the other hand, it could be a strep throat."

"Oh, I hope not," Susie's mother had said with a little downfall of discouragement.

"There's a lot of it around," Dr. Ramsey told her. "You should keep her away from Mathew until we know for sure. It *is* catching, you know."

"How soon can we be sure?" Susie's mother asked.

"Forty-eight hours probably," Dr. Ramsey guessed. "My nurse will call you. In the meantime," he made his pale blue chicken scratch on a little printed prescription form, "start this and we'll see."

Whatever Susie took every four hours did something funny to the inside of her head. A faint, far humming that was a little sickening started inside there, muffling the sounds of her parents' voices when they came to talk to her.

That night Susie could tell that her older sister Carrie had fixed her supper tray. The tray looked like Carrie. On a pale pink place mat was a single spray of daphne in a wine glass trimmed with a ribbon. Her napkin was one of the rose-colored ones that were really sort of worn out, but that was all right because they never used them except on St. Valentine's Day. Her mother always pushed them flat when she laid them out, saying absently, "I must remember to replace these. Why, they used to be red." But she never did buy new ones. In fact Susie rather liked the way the white of the fabric seemed to show through the faded color in thin, crossed lines.

No matter how pretty the tray was, the food didn't have any taste at all and her throat hurt when she tried to swallow it. After scraping off the whipped cream because it made the roof of her mouth all slick and oily, Susie ate the red jello. And she drank her milk.

She didn't even remember who came and got the tray because right away her eyelids became very heavy and she drifted off to sleep.

But the sleep was different. Susie decided that sleep was like eating, if you slept too much you spoiled it for yourself. She drifted awake in the cool dark listening to the house talk to itself, the brush of the shrubs against her window wall and the faint sigh of the furnace clicking itself on. Sometimes she heard dimly the cry of a night bird, lonely and far off, as if it were calling with no hope of an answering voice.

After the results of the test came, the medicine was changed and Susie was bound to the limits of her room for sure.

Through the mornings she would listen to records or do needlework and watch the sunlight move across the wall on the other side of the room. The shaft of light moved almost furtively, as if it were on a secret errand. Slowly it made its way from one of her treasures to another, as if searching for something. After playing gently on her circus poster, it moved on to Henry the Elephant, growing dim with discouragement as it shifted and moved on again.

The mockingbird that always came in late winter perched on the laurel tree outside her window. Everyone liked that bird except Frump, Carrie's white Persian cat. The bird could sing any other bird's song just perfectly, and he sang them one after another like a medley on a record. But when Frump was in the yard, the mockingbird behaved differently. He would mew like a cat and flash in the nectarine tree luring Frump. Then he would dive-bomb the cat, pecking furiously, so that Frump would race to the house to sit sullenly inside the window glaring at the preening bird.

She discovered that the time of day in the house told itself in a series of succeeding sounds. After the silence of his morning nap, her baby brother Mathew would waken with a rhythmic cry. She could barely hear her mother's low voice in response. Against the banging of his toys in the playpen, she felt as well as heard the low vibrating of the vacuum on the living room rug turning suddenly loud and offensive in the hallway just outside her door.

For the first time she noticed that Frump had a schedule all his own. After a night out, he would come to her room, still licking his face from breakfast. He slept there at the foot of her bed, making a marvelous extra warm place until a little after lunchtime. Then he would yawn and stretch and go to the kitchen where she could hear him complaining to Mother about the kibbles in his bowl.

The very first afternoon after she found out for sure she had strep throat, Susie finished one library book and started on the next one. The second book was about Helen Keller. Susie found that the story made her want to cry. But once she started it, she couldn't put it down.

She was still reading it when she heard Carrie's voice coming in from school and Mathew's delighted squeal at her coming. There was something strange about Carrie's arrival though. Usually when Carrie came home, her boyfriend Martin brought her in his little sports car. They would sit there a while and talk, and then Susie would hear the large *RRRRum, RRRRum,* more like a motorcycle than a regular car. That day she heard no motor sound at all outside and wondered if Carrie and Martin were "mad" again.

She looked out the window to see if maybe Martin's car was still there, but the street was empty. The streetlights came on as she looked. It was late. The light had

gone from the sky and the day with it, almost without her knowing it.

The days and nights wove into each other. She read the Helen Keller book again. This time she pretended to be Helen herself instead of the teacher and found herself crying that night from frustration and self-pity.

Dr. Ramsey had promised Susie that she could go back to school when her temperature stayed at 98.6° for forty-eight hours.

"When will that be?" Susie asked.

"Oh," he frowned off into the corner of the office. "Say four or five days maybe, but I won't promise."

When the fifth day had passed and the thin line in the thermometer still wavered up and down, Susie didn't think too much about it, but at the end of the week she was really unhappy. Her throat didn't hurt at all anymore, but that funny, fuzzy feeling was still in her head and her knees ached when she tried to stand up.

Dr. Ramsey came to the house to see her, which was really unusual. He pulled her white desk chair over by her bed and sat down.

"You do remember that I didn't make any promises about going back to school," he reminded her. "Complications can happen. And a few weeks of rest won't do you any harm."

"Weeks," she cried, her voice coming out in a strange

high squeak. "But what about my friends, and school?"

He patted her back down against her pillow. "You can keep up with your schoolwork right here in bed," he assured her. "Mathew and Carrie can come in and out. Your friends can even visit if they don't overdo it."

Somehow Susie blinked back the tears that she felt behind her eyes at his words; but after her mother left to show him to the door, she turned over and cried on her pillow a long time. She listened for Carrie to come home because sometimes Carrie was very understanding to talk to. But Carrie was late that day, and Susie could tell from the way her voice sounded talking to their mother and the way her door shut with a crack that it wasn't going to be a good day to try to talk with her sister.

At least Dr. Ramsey was right about the homework. The very next day Susie's best friend Lindy came by with Susie's books. The teacher had written little notes on slips of yellow paper and stuck them into the pages where the makeup assignments were. Lindy didn't stay very long that day nor the next day either when she came to bring a giant get well card that the class had made. Lindy told her that they had spent a whole art class working on it. The card was so big that it covered her whole bulletin board. By craning her head this way and that Susie could read all the notes the different kids had written and see the funny sketches that the boys had drawn with only their names scratched underneath.

The people at her father's office had a plant sent out on the truck from the florist's. They had planted a thick piggy-back in a pink straw basket trimmed with ribbons. Her father hung it in the window by Susie's bed so that she could watch the sun slide off its curled leaves in the afternoon.

Lindy came by twice the first week and only once the second. That time Susie was sleeping when she came so she didn't get to see her. It troubled Susie that when Lindy was there they seemed to have nothing to talk about. Lindy's mind seemed to be on something else, but when Susie asked her, she only shook her head and said, "It's just that there's nothing to tell you about, that's all."

Lindy always went off with her family over the Easter holidays. A couple of other girls came one afternoon, and they played some games and one of her friends from church choir called and talked a lot about the special services they had had and all. But it was lonesome.

Susie kept wishing her sister's boyfriend Martin would come by. They had been friends for ever so long, even if he did always call her Runt. Martin was such a good, easy person to talk to and they used to play games together when he visited Carrie before. But it was obvious to Susie now that he and Carrie were "on the offs," as he had described it once. That would also explain why Carrie herself was so quiet and unhappy looking, staying off in her room all the time she was home instead of spending any time with Susie.

When Lindy didn't come by again after the holidays and a strange girl from the eighth grade started bringing the assignments by the house, Susie told herself that no matter how it seemed now, everything would be all right again when she was able to go back to school.

So the days dragged themselves into weeks. The Helen Keller book was renewed, and Susie read it two more times along with some other books her mother picked out. These she read only to be polite because her mother was trying so hard. Finally, after what seemed like forever, she was allowed to walk about every day and get her strength up towards starting back to school.

When she got sick, the calendar in the kitchen had a picture of a red-headed boy running and looking back at a kite he was pulling. Now there was a fat brunette girl with ridiculous curls gathering flowers for a May basket.

Mathew, who had been bumping around on the floor, had discovered his legs and hauled his sturdy body up to claw at the table tops with sticky fingers.

When Susie first came out of her room on unsure, skinny legs, the house seemed to have grown and changed. Outside on the patio the lilac bush that Susie had helped her father plant had burst into a foaming of lavender blossoms. And the feel of the house was different. Something chill and fearful seemed to move about the rooms. Maybe she was imagining it. Maybe she was the one who had changed. But in any case, her family's words seemed to come from far off and have meanings that they weren't saying. She felt as if she didn't belong any more, as if she had become a stranger in this familiar place.

Lindy

FINALLY, unbelievably, the day came when Susie
was to go back to school. That morning Susie was
the last one to slip into her chair at breakfast. Her
mother was already spooning cereal into Mathew's open
mouth, and seemed to be distracted, as if her mind were
on something else.

She even forgot to hold Mathew's bowl. When he
tipped it off the high chair tray, a great swoop of that
awful gray stuff splashed clear across the dining room.
Susie's mother didn't laugh, instead she cleaned up the
mess in a tight-lipped silence.

Her father seemed to be reading the paper as usual, but Susie saw his eyes move with concern from his wife to Carrie and back again. Finally he laid down his paper with a sigh.

"Let's just wait," he said softly. "We'll talk about it tonight."

"About what?" Susie asked.

Carrie shot her a knife-edged look, and Susie's mother spoke quickly. "Some of Carrie's business," she said.

"You won't wear it, though?" her mother asked Carrie in a stiff, quiet whisper.

"Is a ribbon around my neck all right?" Carrie asked saucily. "Like a second-grader?"

"Until tonight," her father said firmly.

Then, as if the questions burning in Susie's mind had suddenly blazed up and caught his attention, he looked at her and smiled.

"You still look awfully peaked to me," he commented.

"Her freckles have faded," Carrie said, glancing at Susie, then glancing away quickly. "Maybe they'd all go away if she stayed out of the sun."

It was all right for Carrie to talk about other people's freckles, Susie thought resentfully. Carrie was blonde like Mother with no brown at all in her skin except in the dead of summer when she turned a pale golden color.

"I like freckles," Susie said suddenly. "Maybe I'll just live outside until I turn into one big freckle."

"A five-foot freckle," her father grinned. "That would be interesting."

"Interesting?" Carrie echoed with a faint rise in her voice. Susie knew how Carrie felt about looking interesting. Carrie just wanted to be perfect and beautiful. She did dumb things to herself all the time, but nothing changed her. The stuff from bottles she rubbed on, the way she brushed her hair with her head upside down, even sleeping with a funny little pair of cloth glasses with goo inside didn't help or hinder. Carrie always looked the same with that fine pale hair looking loose and wind-caught on her shoulders and her face smooth and perfect like a flower.

I have a long neck too, Susie told herself defensively. But even as she poked fiercely at her grapefruit, she knew her own long neck was brown that went white all of a sudden where her t-shirt stopped, and two hard round bones stuck up there like apricot pits under her skin.

"She still looks pale to me, too," Susie's mother agreed, setting Mathew on the floor with a cookie in his hand. "But Dr. Ramsey thought it was good to start back on Friday. Then she can rest the weekend and start fresh again Monday."

"Just don't hesitate to come home if you get to feeling tired," her father cautioned, his eyes still concerned.

"I promise," she told him, smiling at him, feeling warm inside as she always did when he looked at her, really looked at her like that.

Ever since kindergarten, Susie had walked to school with Lindy. She thought about calling before she left, but decided she didn't need to. After all, the whole sick thing was over now, and she would just act as if it had never happened. She walked around the block the wrong way just like old times to go past Lindy's house.

She was only halfway to Lindy's when she wished she had called. Thinking about it slowed her steps. Then a strange hesitation like a chill wind struck her as she stood on Lindy's familiar porch, pushing the doorbell like before.

When Lindy's mother opened the door, she looked astonished. "Why, look who's here," she cried as if Susie had been gone forever. "My goodness, child, you look like a ghost." Then with her always a-little-too-loud voice, she called back into the house. "Lindy, Susie Spinner is here."

Her words hit Susie so strangely that she flushed. Susie Spinner. What had happened to just plain Susie in those few weeks?

Lindy came into the living room with a difficult look on her face, as if she knew something secret and not for sharing. Her hair was changed, caught up in front so that the curly ends were loose around her collar. Susie would have sworn she had something on her mouth, not lipstick maybe but something glossy and pale pink that changed her face.

"Gee, Susie," Lindy began, "I'm sorry."

"That's okay," Susie said quickly, thinking about how long it had been since she had seen Lindy. "I knew you must be busy, with the vacation in there and all."

"No," Lindy corrected her. "I mean about this morning. I promised." Her voice trailed off. She glanced at her mother as if for help.

"Now that's silly," Mrs. Farrell said swiftly, careful not to meet Susie's eyes. "There's no reason that the three of you can't walk to school together. Now is there?" she challenged Lindy.

"Of course not," Lindy said after a heavy second. "That is, if she *wants* to."

It had happened too quickly for Susie. Before she could figure it out she saw Trevor Lammers standing in the open door behind her.

A scared feeling hit Susie. She was always afraid when she saw Trevor Lammers outside of school. She was scared of him, and Lindy had always been scared of him, too. They'd talked about it, lots of times, and when they were in their tree at the park and he came with his brothers or his buddies, they always sneaked off home for fear he would pick on them. All the Lammers boys were mean to smaller kids, even the old one who was in Carrie's class; but Trevor was the meanest one of all. Susie still couldn't stand to think of the Jamison cat that he had hung that time so that old Mr. Jamison had found it stiff with agony when he went out to look for it.

But Lindy didn't look afraid now. Instead she was looking at Trevor in that kind of dimpled way that Carrie looked at Martin.

And Trevor wasn't acting bullyish. In fact he was stiffly polite as he spoke to Lindy's mother.

"Hi, Mrs. Farrell," he said in that heavy voice that always sounded too old to Susie. "Is Lindy ready?"

Anybody could tell that Lindy was ready, Susie thought disgustedly. But something about the way she curved her arm when she slid into her jacket and the way she laughed softly when no one had said anything funny made Susie feel sick to her stomach.

When they had walked outside, Susie still stood in the hall staring.

"Let's go if we're going," Trevor said curtly, as if he didn't think it was such a good idea anyway.

The little shove Mrs. Farrell gave Susie was not mean or ugly, but it was a shove. "Run along, friends," she said airily as if she didn't notice a single thing.

That was the most awful walk Susie had ever had in her whole life. She felt out of place and extra. There was no way for three people to walk together on that narrow sidewalk and Trevor and Lindy stayed close as if they were glued together. For a while Susie walked behind, and once after the corner, she was ahead for a while.

And nobody talked. It was as if Susie, just by walking along there, had put a spell of silence on Lindy and Trevor.

A spell of silence. Susie held her lips together hard and looked the other way when they parted at school. Inside herself she felt something fluttering slower and slower as if it were slowly drying in that dark place.

Beyond the Meadow

IF IT HADN'T been for Lindy acting so silly with Trevor and if things hadn't been so strange and tense at home between her mother and Carrie, Susie would never have found her special place at all.

After school there was no one to walk home with. Susie had her arms piled up with extra books for homework when she came out. Lindy and Trevor had already started towards Lindy's house together.

Susie stood undecided for a while. She couldn't stand to trail along a block or so behind them. She could imagine them looking back at her and giggling. Anyway, they might stop and she could catch up with them without meaning to, which would be even worse.

Hitching her books up closer, Susie decided to find a long way to walk home. She walked along Walnut and then turned off on Magnolia. Magnolia had a few houses that were kind of rundown, and on the corner were businesses. Above Magnolia there were only a couple of houses because that's where the Clary land began.

Susie had heard about the Clarys all her life, but she had never known any of them. There had been a bunch of boys and one girl, but they were all lots older. Old Mr. Clary was famous for being a real crosspatch. He was sick a long time before he died, and they offered him lots of money for his farm, which he was too sick to run, but he always said no.

"The day may come when old Clary will be hailed as a hero," she had heard her father say. "Those developers can't seem to cover these hills fast enough, but old Clary has sure held them back."

And he was right. The Clary land was an open meadow that rose in a long curved line to the trees that crowned its crest. From the other side of the hill you could barely see the chimneys of the Clary house peering above the meadow grass.

Susie was almost to the corner of Magnolia and Pine,

still staring up at the Clary land, when she heard someone call her name.

It was Martin, Carrie's boyfriend. He left his work at the service station to cross the street and talk to her.

Martin was very tall, as tall as Susie's father, only skinnier. When he talked to Susie, he cocked his head at her like the shore birds that fed along the marshes. But his dark eyes were always warm-looking. Even though he didn't talk much, Susie always felt like he liked her. He was wiping grease from his hands with a blue cloth as he grinned down at her.

"Hey, Runt," he said. "I haven't seen you for a while."

"I've been sick," she told him. "Didn't Carrie tell you?"

Strangely he didn't look at her. Instead he glanced at the Clary meadow above the station. Susie followed his eyes to where the wild green meadow rose to disappear into a clump of dark trees. But he wasn't thinking about the meadow because he said, "Carrie hasn't been doing much talking to me lately."

"Are you mad?" she asked curiously.

"I'm not mad," he replied, grinning a funny way. "But I think she's crazy." He heard a horn at the station and looked back. "Oops, my master's voice." He thumped her on the head as he left. "Don't forget your old friends," he cautioned as he loped back across the street to his work.

Susie stood a minute staring up at where Martin had looked, wondering about him and Carrie. They had gone together for so long now that it was hard to imagine any quarrel lasting forever. Was it being mad at Martin that had made Carrie so cross and solitary these past weeks? Somehow that didn't seem likely. When Martin and Carrie had broken up other times, her mother and father hadn't paid any attention, and Carrie and her mother certainly hadn't ever had any cross words about it. She puzzled over this, walking slower and slower.

Susie dreaded getting home. Her mother was bound to ask about Lindy because Lindy had always come home with her after school. Lindy's mother was a big golfer who played every afternoon it didn't rain. For years Lindy had always come home and had a snack with Susie even if she wasn't going to stay and play. That way Lindy's mother didn't worry about her being at home alone so much.

Susie didn't want her mother to ask about Lindy until she had figured out for herself what was going on with Lindy and Trevor.

Susie wasted all that dreading. Her mother didn't even notice that Lindy hadn't come along. In fact, her mother didn't seem to be noticing much of anything. Mathew was in the backyard in his playpen banging and bouncing about, but her mother was just sitting there on the step in the sun staring past the lilac bush.

As Susie sat down, her mother slipped an arm around her without even looking.

Frump, who had been sunning on the empty dog-house where Starchy used to sleep, jumped down to join them. He rubbed against Susie's shoulder, butting her with his flat head. Then he draped his tail across Susie's face so that her nose prickled.

"Have a nice day?" her mother asked.

"It was okay," Susie said. "How about you?"

Before her mother could answer, Susie heard the phone ring in the kitchen. She hadn't even realized that Carrie was home until she heard Carrie's footsteps racing through the house. Carrie answered the phone before her mother got there.

Because her mother was standing there in the door listening, Susie listened too. Carrie's voice was rich and funny, not like her usual voice at all. She just said "hello," and laughed a little, a funny way and then said, "Just a minute, I'll go to the other phone."

Carrie didn't look at at either of them as she left the kitchen. She just unplugged the hall phone and took it into her own room and shut the door.

Maybe the closed door made Susie's mother restless. After a minute she hung up the kitchen phone and started stirring around the kitchen even though it was really too early to start dinner.

After a while she came to the back door as if she had just that minute remembered about Susie. "Don't feel that you have to sit out there and watch Mathew, Susie," she said. "You could run out and play if you feel good enough. It's an awfully pretty afternoon."

Susie wanted to cry. Where would she go? Who would she play with? She thought of other afternoons. She and Lindy had a special tree in the corner of the park near the tennis court. They used to sit there and watch people and talk. Sometimes they had shared a Cherry Sloopy, rich-tasting red syrup on chipped ice. But that was only if one of them had some allowance left.

The tree in the park wasn't a place you would want to go to by yourself.

Because it was easier to go off than to explain staying home, Susie rose listlessly. "I'll be back in a little while," she told her mother halfheartedly.

"Just don't be late for supper," her mother replied, her voice still kind of faraway and funny.

When Susie took her green sweater out of her room, she could hear Carrie's voice rising and falling behind the closed door.

Without even thinking, Susie started towards the grassy hill that rose beyond the station where Martin worked. First she had to pass a row of houses that moved like stairsteps up the grade.

Dogs barked from behind fences at her, and she

thought of her own dog Starchy who had died the year she was in the third grade. Susie and her father had wanted another dog, but her mother had been very stubborn.

"It hurts too much," she said. "I don't want to have to go through that again."

In a way Susie understood, but in another way it was almost like telling Starchy that all the fun of having him wasn't worth the crying when he was gone. She squatted by a fence and whistled softly to a pair of dachshunds. They tried to get their noses through the slats of the fence to her; their fat bodies waggled wildly. The smaller one whimpered and started jumping against the fence as she walked on.

The meadow grass was tall and thick. It whooshed against her legs as she walked, springing back crisply. There were so many smells. She thought about Helen Keller again. How would it be to smell that thick dusty smell or the fine giddy scents of herbs and not to know how they looked or even what they were called?

She decided to try how it would be there alone on the hills. When she shut her eyes tight, the smells grew suddenly stronger, the strangest sounds she hadn't even noticed before stirred in the air all about her. She held her hands out before herself a little warily for fear she might run into something. Behind the red darkness of her eyelids, she was in a private threatening world. She walked a long time, stumbling sometimes on the uneven ground.

Then suddenly her hand struck something hard. Her eyes shot open. She was at the edge of the woods. The trees were not like trees in people's yards, set apart with grass between. They stood close together like a wall; like the hedge that surrounded the sleeping beauty, she thought. She stared into the darkness of the grove a long time. The trees weren't solid in there; instead they stood in a rough oval about a clearing. She could tell that no tree had died there because there was no stump in the middle, only pale soft green that looked starved for sun.

It was easy enough to tell that this was a special place. Outside in the meadow the grasses swayed and stirred with the wind of afternoon, but the grass in this place was still, as if it were frozen in an attitude of waiting. No dragonflies hung above the blossoms as they did in the meadow, and the birds that twitched in the circle of trees were invisible, hidden among the mysterious twisting of the gnarled branches.

As Susie stared into the clearing she felt a strange breathlessness that she remembered from other special times.

When she had been very small and still full of the stories her mother read to her, she used to look for those green rings where fairies came to dance at night.

Then, long after she gave up believing in magic, she

had found such a ring. The grass had been tender and pale like this grass. It had gleamed with dew caught in delicate strands of spider webs. A circle of tiny toadstools had enclosed the place as if they were sentries.

She had instantly known that, whether she believed in fairies or not didn't matter: their spirits lived in the place; and she had walked out of her way to avoid trespassing.

Since then there had been other places . . . a secret cave on her grandparents' farm where a pure-hearted old Indian chief was said to have come to die. Her grandfather had a whole case of arrowheads and relics like that, but he would never let anyone disturb the dust of that cave. His rich loud voice fell to softness when he took her there, as if he could feel as she did, the gentle spirit that still stirred in the dim green air of that place.

Whatever spirit lived in this grove of trees was a gentle spirit too; Susie was sure of that. More than anything she wanted to become one with the spirit of the grove, but she would have to be inside the circle of rustling trees for that to happen.

Susie had never been quite so careful before. She moved so slowly that a green-tailed lizard on an exposed root didn't even flick away as she passed him. Very carefully she folded back the branches of the tree that blocked her passage. Not one leaf must be twisted nor a twig bent, she told herself solemnly. She must come and go with no sign of passing, or the grove would banish her forever.

She even knew how the grove would shut her out. The leaves that now turned gently in the wind in a kind of whispering welcome would fit closely, one upon another like protecting hands, to hide their private place. The morning glory vines, whose naked stems tendrilled and wove about the tree roots, would grow massive and forbidding, weaving a net to hold her out.

Once inside the enclosure, she knew that she must not press the moist pale green grass lest it wound the spirit of the place. In a faint obeisance to this spirit, she found a low gray rock, trimmed with a sturdy lace of lichen. Her tailbone hurt because of her thinness, but the longer she sat and the quieter she waited, the more the place approved of her.

There was a music she could hear only in special places. Sitting there she invited the music to herself. The music began softly just beyond her ear, a rising and falling like a child's voice in solitude, like the wordless crooning of Mathew when he curled in the crib playing with his toys and winding down to sleep. The music came from inside herself moving through the mysterious passages of her body, thrumming in the cavern where her heart hung, singing gently along her veins.

Maybe it was because she had been playing Helen Keller in the meadow, maybe it was a special something about the grove. For whatever reason she knew within herself that the grove was a place of silence.

"I will never speak here," she promised herself faithfully. "Here I will always be mute, like the trees."

As if in approval of her pledge, the thrumming inside herself grew stronger and louder. She almost had to hold her breath because of the wonder of it.

The Visitor

THE MUSIC that wove all about her ceased suddenly like a candle going out. Susie caught her breath sharply for she knew that she was not alone any more. The music never came when any other large creature was near. Without moving her head, she searched the circle of bushes and trees to see who had joined her so secretly.

At first she thought he was a cat because he was not much bigger than Frump. His face was a burnished red and along his jaws a patterning of white moved up to

line his high-pricked ears. He had whiskers like a cat though, coal black whiskers, very stiff looking, brisk and efficient against the softness of his fur.

His eyes were as brown as her own, lined with black as if they had mascara on them. But the black of his pupils seemed larger than necessary as he stared at her fixedly without moving from her gaze.

His nose was a single black gleaming coal, and he wore no expression at all. We are looking at each other, Susan told herself silently. The fox and I are looking at each other, and I must not move first. A faint acrid scent filled her head so that her eyes swam with tears, but she did not move. Instead the smell itself made her giddy.

I smell the fox and the fox smells me, she thought with an unreasoning excitement. And I am not afraid.

As if she had challenged him, the fox rose to his feet. His legs were slender as the stems of flowers under the bushiness of his coat. He was crouched only a little, as if to spring very fast if she should threaten him. In that half-bent way, his great brush of a tail level with his back, he moved across the center of the clearing, his eyes never leaving hers for a moment. Then he was gone into the shadows of the brush as silently as he had come.

Time, which had ceased while the music sounded and the fox's eyes were on her own, suddenly began to tick in the air of the clearing. It was not the ticking of a clock nor the restless impatience of her mother's voice but only the memory of both in the click of an insect and the knowledge of the guilt she would feel at being late.

The fox is not the spirit of this place, she told herself. When I come again, and again, and again, maybe I shall meet it.

She backed out of the opening she had come through. Just at the edge where the trees straggled to an end and the grasses began, she dropped to one knee quickly, only for an instant. Maybe the spirit would see that and welcome her back.

She ran very fast down the meadow to home, whipping her legs with the long grasses. But her mother didn't even seem to realize it was late. She was talking to her father in the kitchen, holding Mathew who fretted and scolded in her arms.

They stopped talking the moment Susie came in, as if they were afraid of her hearing them.

Then her father smiled and touched her hair. "Hey, Susie," he asked softly, "would you mind watching this pest a few minutes for your Mom? Outside in the play-pen would be fine."

Mathew fought his sweater until he realized she was taking him outdoors, then he clapped his hands and shouted in those funny noises he used for happy. Her parents kept on talking, low and unhappy. Even though she didn't hear the names, Susie knew it was something about Carrie.

She shut their voices from her ears concentrating on Mathew.

Mathew liked to eat ants. This was so astonishing to Susie that she watched him for a few minutes in silence without stopping him. It was very clever the way he caught them. He licked his fat finger and carefully thrust his hand through the bars of the playpen. Gingerly he put his wet finger on a column of ants. Two or three would catch on his wet finger, wriggling. He would pop the finger into his mouth, roll his tongue about a little, look delighted, and start again.

Susie glanced at the half-open patio door. She knew absolutely that eating ants would be one of the things she was supposed to stop, but a sudden giggle of curiosity struck her. She grinned at Mathew, licked her finger and caught an ant for herself. As a matter of fact there were two. They had a prickly, slightly sweetish taste on her tongue. Then she realized what she had done and raced to the hose to wash her mouth out.

"No," she said to Mathew, moving the playpen so the ants were too far for him to reach. But she whispered as if he would tattle on her. He whimpered a moment in protest, but when she rolled his ball to him, the one with the bright fishes caught inside, he grinned and grabbed it and forgot.

Her walk had made her dozy. She leaned back in the grass, staring at the tiny fruit just forming on the nectarine tree. From inside she could hear her parents' voices rise. But maybe she'd been wrong, they weren't talking about Carrie at all. At least they didn't say her name.

"What about Angelica Clary?" she heard her mother ask almost triumphantly. "Would you say that she made the most of her life?"

"Who knows, Martha?" he asked sharply. "You certainly aren't going to blame her early death on an early marriage are you?"

"No, but that man."

"You won't get me to say anything against Douglas Born," he said flatly. "He's raised that boy by himself, asking no help from the Clarys at all. And now that old Mrs. Clary is sick, who is it that's come to take care of her? Doug Born, that's who."

"You're kidding," she said with amazement.

"Not a bit of it," he said shortly. "I have to admit I was as surprised as you when I realized who it was. I only knew that one of the kids had come to take over after that last fall of hers. But it's not one of her own boys. It's Doug Born."

"But the boy, where is he?"

"He's with him, up there at the Clary place."

"But shouldn't he be in school?"

"Probably," her father said mildly. "But the ox is in the ditch. And after the way the good townspeople acted when Angelica and Doug ran away, I wouldn't expect him to turn a half-grown boy loose among their tongues. Would you?"

Her mother's voice was low and contrite, so quiet that Susie couldn't catch the words.

In only a little while her father came to the door. "Let's bring that fellow in, Susie," he said. "His dinner is ready now."

Susie sniffed with pleasure as she carried Mathew in. The smell of roasted chicken and the sharpness of sage battled with the scent of onion. She knew there would be cranberry sauce, the canned, jellied kind. She liked watching her mother open the can at both ends, letting the jelly slide out on the leaf-shaped dish to be cut into round slices still bearing the marks of the can.

But now Mathew was eating, banging the high chair tray with two round fists, both holding spoons. Meanwhile her mother was slipping neat, rounded spoonsful of that thick fine stuff into his open mouth as fast as it slid down his throat. Once in a while he would remember to sputter, spraying the tray and the air and her mother with a fine, dark, shower of food.

Susie needed to share her fox, but it was too big a thing to share with more than one person. She needed a private sharing.

She stared at her father's face until his eyes slid from his paper to her face. Absently he leaned towards her, lifting a strand of her dark hair from her face.

"Something, Susan?" he asked quietly.

"I saw a fox today," she said very quietly.

"A red fox or a gray fox?" he asked curiously.

"Not really red," she said thoughtfully. "More a rich brownish. But it was shady. In the sun he might have been red."

"What was he doing?"

She grinned at him, hoping he'd understand. "Looking at me."

He laughed softly. "And you stayed like that until the cock crowed?"

"He got tired of looking first," she said, trying to hide her pride. "Then he walked away, still looking."

He nodded. "Off on a fox's business, I suppose."

"He smelled," she told him.

"That close?" he said wonderingly. "He must have trusted you."

"I didn't move at all," she explained.

"You won't believe this, but we are finally ready to eat," her mother called from the kitchen beyond.

Her father heaped the paper on the table all in a pile and caught Susie by the elbow, pulling her up.

"I'm just glad you weren't a fat hen or a gaggly goose."

She was all the way to the table before she realized what he meant. Then she pushed the idea away from her mind fast. She would not think of her fox with his fine muzzle stained with blood and feathers. He was a special fox, not a hunter or a killer. He was the fox of the clearing.

Then she noticed that there were only three places set.

When she glanced up at her mother's face, it reddened in a funny way.

"Carrie said she isn't hungry tonight," her mother explained quickly.

Her father started talking about something else very fast as if to make their minds go away from the place where Carrie usually sat.

Becoming Native

CARRIE STAYED in her room with the door closed all day Saturday. Somehow having Carrie's door closed made the house quieter to Susie, as if the very boards of the walls were listening and waiting. Each hour took a very long time to pass. Susie did all the makeup work she had been assigned, except for the science. For one thing the science assignment looked awfully hard, and it wasn't going to be due for a week or two more.

While her mother went shopping, Susie watched

Mathew and read the science assignment through again.

Select one of the following: Native trees, native shrubs, native flowers, native mammals, song birds of the Bay Area, water birds of the Bay area. Study several examples within the category you have chosen, draw and describe them, giving their proper names, and explain their use in the balance of nature.

Susie had to admit to herself that the grove was where she wanted to go. But she was afraid. What if she went again and the grove turned out not to be special at all, but only a bunch of scraggly old trees with thick grass between? Then she had a great idea. If she went there to do wild flowers for her science project, then it wouldn't be so awfully hard. She could tell herself that she had only gone for the assignment anyway. Even if the grove was not special, she would have something for her pictures when she got home.

She went off as soon as her mother came back. She wanted to play Helen Keller again in the meadow and see if the spirit of the place would lead her right to the grove, but she was afraid it might not. Instead she watched the grasses as she passed and picked three flowers to draw in the blue spiral notebook she brought with her.

The meadow was different on a cloudy afternoon.

The grove, when she passed into it, was almost dark. Susie stared at the well of darkness between the trees. Long ago she had been afraid of darkness, but now that seemed silly to her. The darkness was there all the time even when the sun came high and brilliant trying to seek it out. But the darkness only hid from the sun beneath stones and on the backs of trees and under outcroppings of earth. The darkness was native, and the sun was only a passing traveller.

Mathew had come from darkness. She remembered how he blinked at the light those first few days. "It was dark where he came from," her father explained.

I came from darkness too, she reminded herself as she parted the branches on the secret place. It's natural to me, and that's why I'm not scared.

But even in the dimness of the shadowed grove there was a white flower that seemed to have found some light of its own. It gleamed as she knelt to stare at it. Painfully, line by line, she drew a small picture of it, leaving plenty of space underneath to put in the name when she found out what it was.

She was still there, half on her knees, when she felt rather than heard the sweep through the air. The movement was silent as a moth, but the air fanned against her face as if the moth were giant with soft wings wider than a man.

Her heart thumped with terror, and she crouched very low.

Was this the spirit ruler? Was he a giant moth who came from the shadows to this private place?

When the air grew still, she looked up awkwardly, carefully, for fear she might see something she did not wish to meet with her eyes.

The grove was empty and silent. Very slowly she stared all about her, at the bushiness of shrubs and at the branches of the trees.

When she saw the eyes of the owl, she held very still. His deep brown eyes were fixed on her, seeming to search the smallest dark corner of her mind. He was the tallest bird she had ever seen, taller than a gull even, but his body was blocky and oval shaped, with stripes running from his flat face to the cruel bright claws of his feet.

He had no tufty ears like the owls in pictures. Instead a fluffy ring of feathers framed his face like a mane on a lion.

Susie wanted the owl to speak. If the owl were indeed the spirit of this place, then he would speak to her.

But the owl only tired of looking at her. With a dignity that made her feel almost wormlike, he turned his head to the side and stared into the trees as if he were bored with her presence.

She left the grove quickly, glancing back for fear that the wide soft wings of the owl might drift there above her, starting goose pimples of terror along her arms.

But once she was in the open meadow, she was suddenly filled with happiness. She danced wildly, throwing her arms every which way.

It's a sign, she told herself gleefully, a sure-enough sign. The owl was like the fox, special for that special place. I am accepted, she told herself. I really am accepted.

When she got home she copied her sketch from the spiral notebook onto the drawing paper and looked it up in the flower book. She colored the sketch with the pencils that Carrie had given her two Christmases before, which were too special to use on just any drawing. The pale, whitish flower with tiny lilac-colored veins was called a milkmaid. She carefully copied down its real name, *Dentaria Californica*. She wrote down that the root of the plant was good to eat and had a slightly peppery taste and that it was kin to a radish. She was still leafing through the flower book curiously when she noticed that some of the plants were called "alien." She had to think a minute where she had last heard that word used about something else.

Then she remembered Lore. They had talked about an alien being someone like Lore who came from away.

It startled Susie to realize that some of the flowers were alien to the grove and the meadow even as she herself was. But the flowers had made their home there finally, fitting naturally in among the blades of native grass, as Lore had gradually fitted in, becoming just one of the kids.

Lore had come to Susie's school from Bremen in Germany. She was a thick, warm person with fine soft hair that grew under her regular hair so that when the sun was behind her, Susie could see a pale circle of light hanging around her head. When Susie had smiled at her the first time, Lore had studied Susie's face a long minute before she smiled back, as if she had to be sure whether it was the right thing to do or not.

Lore's dresses were longer than the other girls' and also a little bigger around. It was as if her mother had been thinking of someone else when she bought them, someone a little older, maybe, who had grown in all directions.

The teacher called her Laurie, but on the board the name was spelled funny so that it looked like Lore instead of Laurie.

"Lore is going to become an American citizen," Mrs. Tate told them. "We will all need to help her."

"I got to be a citizen with no help from anybody," Trevor had scoffed.

"Your mother and father can take credit for that, but you really can't," Mrs. Tate told him with a smile. "If it had not been for them, you would have to learn all the things that Lore has to learn and pass a test like she has to."

Susie stared at the sketch of the alien flowers and thought about her secret place. Maybe it was because she had so much to learn of the grove that its spirit never came to her. She could feel its magic all around her, moving even into her lungs making them seem full of air when she hadn't even breathed deep. But she was still an alien. What did she need to know? What tests would she need to pass?

Maybe her clothes were too big and all wrong somehow. She remembered how Lore's dress stood out from her neck so far that Susie could see the small hump of her topmost spine bone, fuzzy with pale, soft hair.

She must find the right clothes for the green kingdom, Susie decided, a special costume so that the spirit would know that she wanted to belong. And learn the language. She remembered Lore stumbling over English words, beet red from blushing.

But for the silent grove there could be no language. There would be only the names of things, like the fox and the owl and the carpet of flowers.

Her clothes were easy enough. She had a pair of old jeans that used to be a deep green color. Now they were almost too small, and faded and yellowish in spots where she had worn them nearly through. She got out a cast-off brown T-shirt that Carrie had given her. She marked on it with a green waterproof marker in big spots, trying to make it look like the mottled green and brown of the tree trunks seen through the leaves. The T-shirt turned out so well that she marked the jeans with brown so they matched. Then between the grass stains of her old tennis shoes she made brown marks with crayon.

When she half-closed her eyes and looked at herself, she seemed like a part of the forest, a wild skinny tree.

She wore the forest-grove clothes out to the backyard where her parents were sitting together talking and watching Mathew. They didn't even notice.

She had stood there a minute waiting, but her father only asked, "What's up with you, Cookie?"

"I just thought I'd go play on the hill awhile," she said lamely.

"Don't be too late," he said absently. "It still gets dark pretty early."

They weren't noticing her because of Carrie, she decided, climbing the hill. Something hurt inside her chest as she parted the trees to enter the grove.

She immediately knew that she had been right about the clothes. The humming of the insects didn't even stop when she came. She sat on her same gray rock and stayed very still. I am one with the grove, she told herself soberly. Sometime, not today maybe, not even by summer, but someday the spirit of the grove would be known to her.

And she would have earned it, with her silence and her being a part of the sorrel and the wild radish and the lupine that lived here today. Her mind stumbled a little on the words, hoping she was pronouncing them right.

Then suddenly the stillness came again. Had they just noticed her, she wondered, or was the fox coming again, or the owl?

She moved her head carefully, trying not to make a sudden jerk. There was nothing at all in the shadowy trees about her. Then she looked at the opening where she had come in. She could feel her breath stop short in her throat. A boy was standing there. A boy larger than herself with unruly long hair and very angry pale blue eyes in a sullen face.

The First Test

THE BOY stood in the opening of the trees with the sun lighting the edges of his clothes. Because his face was in darkness, he looked scarier than he really was, Susie told herself quickly. He stood there a long time, staring at her solemnly as the fox had done. But because he was human like herself, Susie felt strange under his glance. She had to hold herself very tight inside to keep from leaping to her feet and running away wildly through the trees.

He was not looking at her as the fox had, she knew

that. He was not just checking to see if she was dangerous. He was looking to see how she looked, and she felt her face turning red under his eyes. She knew already how she looked. She didn't need him to stare at her to find out.

All the awful things about herself, the things she thought and the things that Carrie had said in anger came back in a rush. She felt the absolute end of ugliness there on the gray rock, too thin and tall with a skin that was spotted with freckles wherever the sun touched.

Her eyes were too large for her face, and her hair, too heavy to stay fastened back with anything, was bunched up in the back.

But even after he had seen all that, he just kept standing there, looking. Finally he spoke almost angrily.

"I don't know why you're here," he said flatly, as if she were trespassing.

It wasn't because of the vow of silence that she had made to the grove, she realized. Maybe she was afraid. Maybe it was just that it wasn't a question but a rude remark and she was not obliged to answer rude remarks. In any case she only slid her eyes from his and stared down at her sneakers with their green grass stains in among the brown spots.

"You've camouflaged yourself," the boy said with a discovering tone. "You expecting enemy planes, maybe?" His voice rose in a sneer, and he took a step closer to her. His eyes were a very pale blue with sort of threads in the colored parts.

"You think you're something, don't you? Sitting there on your silly rock with those crazy clothes not answering anybody?"

She glanced at him and then away quickly. Now she was really scared, something hard and wanting to hurt in his voice made her shiver inside.

"I could make you speak," he threatened. "I could even make you holler. That's what. I'm a green belt in judo, you know." He grabbed her arm hard in his hand and shook her. "I could break you in pieces, you're that much of nothing."

If she cried out, the tears would come, she knew that. So she only wrested her arm away and rubbed it on the bruised place where he had gripped her too hard. But tears swam in her eyes in spite of everything.

Then he stood very close looking at her, and she felt something in him seem to melt, as if his anger bled from him into the grass.

"You're dumb," he said softly with a kind of sense of wonder. "That's what you are, a dumb mute. You CAN'T speak."

She had not meant to look up at him again, but his words startled her.

He looked as if he were delighted. It was as if of all

the things there were in the world, the one he wanted most to find was a wordless person. Why? she wondered, staring at him.

"Can you hear?" he asked a little loudly.

Because the loudness of his voice stilled the woods of birdsong, she nodded to him. Later she wondered why she hadn't answered, but then the moment to speak was somehow gone. Maybe she didn't want to disappoint him, to let him realize that she was as ordinary as she really was.

Suddenly he was friendly. He squatted on his heels so that his eyes were on a level with her own.

"You scared me a little, you know," he admitted. "I thought you were a statue or something. Except that statues don't dress like that." He gestured at the faded green jeans and the brown pullover that used to be Carrie's.

"What do you do here, just sit and watch? Is it 'cause you haven't any friends?"

His gaze was too intense, something hard like waves of energy seemed to strike her as he talked. She slid her eyes from his face and looked away, into the deep green beneath the oak.

"I haven't any friends either," he admitted, picking up a stick and probing at the earth with it. "At least not here. I'm here for just a while though. My friends are all back home. But you LIVE here."

She nodded.

"I'll go back after—" he paused and looked at her almost cunningly. "I have to wait." She sensed that there was something he had meant to say and stopped just short of. Why? Had he thought she might laugh, or be shocked?

If she smiled at him, he would think she wanted him to stay. In a way she did, but in another way she didn't. He would spoil the grove being there. The spirit would never reveal itself with such a loud, bright-colored person with that yellow hair and all.

But she wanted to know where he was from and why he was here and what he was waiting for. She knew she had only to break the silence and ask, but somehow she could not.

He stood there a long minute just looking at her. Then suddenly he started whipping at a tree with the stick he was carrying. It was the hawthorn tree that stood just to the right of where she had seen the fox. As he struck the tree, a shower of spent blossoms fell on the green of the grove floor. The bark was stripping from the tree's branches so that they looked naked and sick.

He's mean, she thought angrily, mean and cruel like Trevor. She stared at him a moment with all the hate she could make her eyes hold, and then she looked away.

"For Cripes sake. It's only a silly old tree," he said resentfully when she turned her face from him.

"Anyway it's my grandmother's land. I can kill everything here if I want to."

She still didn't move. Now she understood. This was the Clary boy, the son of the girl Angelica who had run away and gotten married and died.

She knew he wanted her to look back at him, but she wouldn't.

Instead she folded her hands determinedly and stared at a certain place across the clearing. She stared at it unswervingly without even winking for a long time.

He knew that she had drawn away from him and was annoyed. He rose and stood in front of her so that her eyes were on his shirt button, the third one from the top. She pretended that she could see through it, still staring at the green place she had chosen, not letting her face change.

He reached out as if to strike her on the shoulder but withheld his hand. Then he spoke angrily.

"You're crazy. You're just mad, that's all. You can sit there and be mad all you want to, you don't scare me. My grandmother's mad, and I'm not even afraid of her, so why should I be afraid of you?"

A hard something caught in her throat at his words, but she held her eyes tightly in their place, not moving.

"I got better things to do than sit around here in the dark with a crazy person," he said sullenly. "There's a worse thing than being by yourself."

He threw the stick onto the ground so hard that it bounced in the springy grass before it settled there.

He pushed the branches aside roughly as he went out. From the very corner of her eye, she could see him crossing the meadow. He had snatched a handful of grass and he was striking the air with it. And every few steps he looked back as if she might be following.

When he had completely disappeared from view, she ran all the way home across the dark meadow, wondering if she would ever have the courage to come again.

Simples

SUSIE FELT strangely tired when she got home from the grove. Because Carrie was still shut up in her room, Susie set the table while her mother fed Mathew. After she finished wiping the dishes, she went off to her own room.

By now she knew the beginning of the Helen Keller book by heart, but she found herself caught by it as much as before. It was different to read it now after the silence of the grove and being walled off from Lindy and her family the way she was. She was halfway in tears near the end when her door was opened softly.

"You're still awake," her father said with surprise. "Sally Farrell wants to talk to you on the phone."

Susie frowned. Then she realized. Not Lindy, but Sally. That was Lindy's mother's name.

Mrs. Farrell's voice was not as loud as usual but higher, almost ending in a squeak. "Have you seen Lindy, honey?" she asked quickly.

"No, I haven't," Susie said. "Not since yesterday morning."

"I mean this evening," Mrs. Farrell said impatiently. "Has she been over there since dinner?"

"I haven't seen her at all since Friday morning," Susie said.

After a funny long silence, Mrs. Farrell said crossly, "Now let's get this straight. She wasn't over there last night?"

"No, Mrs. Farrell," Susie replied with a sudden sinking of her heart.

"Very well," Mrs. Farrell snapped, and the phone line went dead in Susie's ear.

"What was all that about?" Susie's father asked curiously from his chair.

"Lindy's mom thought Lindy was with me," Susie said carefully.

"Something wrong with you and Lindy?" her mother asked curiously.

"I just haven't seen her, that's all," Susie said and went back to bed quickly before they asked any more questions.

The phone call nagged at Susie all day Sunday. A kind of funny dread came whenever she thought about it. Finally late Sunday afternoon she decided to go back to the grove and maybe get some more wild flowers while she was there.

The boy's coming was probably just by chance, and even if he came again, she could always leave.

Susie felt like a sneak as she wrapped the papers and her colored pencils in with the wild flower book. What was it they had called the stuff they carried around in the school play . . . props, that was it. She knew that all those things she zipped into the schoolbag were just that, stage props. She was going to the grove for a different reason. It wasn't that she thought she would do anything for her science report. She was running away from a heavy kind of beating inside her chest.

The day that had been bright had grown darker. The whole sky was filled with scudding small clouds that looked like the lamb's wool inside her ice skates. Once in a while the sun would find a place but just for a moment before being covered again. There were flowers in the grass she hadn't seen before, so she picked them as she went.

The secret place grew very still when she entered it.

Then slowly, sound by sound, the rhythm of the place returned, the small rackety hum of insects and the twitter of the small birds that Susie could never quite see. They twitched about in the heavy foliage, as dark as the shadows but no larger than finches.

She had been right to come here; she knew that after only a few minutes. Her scared feeling about Lindy faded away, and she had that smooth calm feeling that she was a part of the deep green.

Then suddenly the song began. Susie had never heard a bird sing like this one did. First the bird sang a single long note as if he were introducing the song with a name. After the smallest kind of a pause, he sang three or four phrases, then paused and sang again in a different tone. By the time he started the third time, she had located him on a branch of the hawthorn across the clearing. Like herself the bird was dressed to disappear in the colors of that place. His back was a soft chocolate brown and his breast pale, with soft brown spots that looked as if water color had been dabbed on and run. Once in a while he would cock his reddish tail and then drop it slowly as if he had forgotten he was supposed to hold it up.

Then the song was over. The bird's voice changed. "Chuck," it said, "tuk-tuk-tuk." Then harshly, "Pay." With a jerk it rose from the branch and was gone.

The boy's voice near her elbow startled Susie.

"That's a hermit thrush," the boy said quietly. "They always say that at the end, 'Pay,' as if you were supposed to throw them money."

It was shivery the way he had come so quietly without her hearing or seeing him. She glanced at where the bird had been and back to him. He was chewing a piece of weed in his mouth like someone in a cowboy movie.

"I knew you were here," he said triumphantly. "I knew because I've been watching with the glasses from my grandmother's house. I saw you coming across the field picking stuff up. What did you get?"

Susie spread a hand protectively over the little pile of wild flowers beside her on the grass. At her movement he moved closer, squatting down to stare at them, but making no move to touch them.

Then he snorted disgustedly. "I know what those are," he said in a superior way. "Those are country simples like my grandmother collected. I know all those and even what they're for." He picked up a stalk of bright green with small, starry flowers clustered about its stem. "That's Solomon's seal," he said. "It makes berries that are used for medicine. That adder's tongue has a root that you eat if you've been poisoned, to make you real sick to get rid of the poison." He picked up another. "And that's red maids whose berries make pinole. You're not half-bad at this stuff, are you?"

Susie stared at her pile of flowers in amazement. Country simples! She'd never even heard the phrase before, and here he knew all about the plants.

At her glance he shrugged and twisted his mouth. "You see, I was right. You are mad just like my grandmother. She did that all her life, collected simples and wrote down about them and even kept them in jars. That's how come she got hurt so bad. She was prowling around out here in the half-dark and fell.

"All night she lay there with a broken hip in the cold. That's why she going to die, because the hip wasn't taken care of till late the next day when somebody came by and found her."

He must have read the sympathy in Susie's face, for he rose suddenly and threw the stem from his mouth hard. "Good enough for her, I'd say. She ought to have just died out there, crying for help."

Susie thought of her own grandmother Spinner living alone on the farm where she and Grandpa had lived ever since her dad was a boy. What if she fell like this boy's grandmother? A lump came quickly to her throat and she shook her head.

Her gesture made him angry. "A lot you know about it. Just a lot you know?" He spoke harshly right in her face, then sensing her fear, pulled away a little as he had that first time. He started to talk, as if he were talking to himself. But he kept saying, "you know," at the end of sentences, so he must have remembered she was there.

He was squatting down a funny way so that he was sitting on his heels. Her father called that hunkering.

She remembered her father using that word, when he was telling her a story.

"Back when I was a boy on the farm," he started, "I got to go in town with my daddy on Saturday to buy supplies. We'd pile the back of the pickup full and then have lunch at the diner. Pie. I always had pie even though my mom made better pies than that diner ever heard of. But their pies looked better, piled high with whipped-cream-looking stuff and dark chocolate inside. When you tasted it, the chocolate part was like sweet gravy and the cream went to fluff, but I still always ordered it.

"After lunch my daddy gave me fifteen cents, ten cents for the show and a nickel for popcorn. Then he'd join the other farmers in front of the feed store. They all sat like this" (he had demonstrated for her), "and my daddy called it hunkering. Any farmer worth his salt can hunker a day and a night without weaving," he told her, winking.

Susie tried hunkering right then, but after only a few minutes one of her feet would go to sleep or she would start teetering. But this boy hunkered as if it felt natural, even good, to him.

67

"She's going to die, my grandmother is," the boy said. "And I don't even care. The dying part is not so hard. I saw a dog die once that was hit by a car. It seemed like he felt better after it was over. The part that's hard about dying is the waiting, you know." He looked at her searchingly, but she only stared back because she didn't understand.

"My mother died," the boy said. His eyes were on the ground away from her; he picked at the grass roots way down where little pale brownish hulls showed as if some blades had tried to make it to green and hadn't managed to. "She was a long time dying. Only one thing she wanted and that was to come back home. Why I'll never know," he said angrily. "This creepy place! But she wanted to come home so bad that she talked about it all the time. Even at night, you know, when she and Dad thought I was asleep I'd hear her talking about the place here. Grandma's place and the field." He pointed. "That one out there. Her secret place." He glanced about the grove with a funny look, then he shrugged.

"You wouldn't believe how rough it was. There wasn't anything that the doctors or us could do. She just kept on dying and there wasn't anything she wanted to eat and she was too weak to do anything. The only thing in the whole world she wanted was to come home. And would they let her? Not on your life. Talk about mean!

"Dad even called long distance telling them that Angelica wanted to come home to see her mother, but the old man, my grandfather, just took the phone and hung it up.

"And my mom didn't even get mad. She just put her hand on my dad's arm and said, 'Don't blame Mom, it's not her. Dad just isn't one for forgiving.'"

The boy paused; his restless hands were suddenly quiet. Susie could see the anger coming again in his changeable face. "I don't care how hard Grandmother's dying is; I just don't care."

Then he did a strange thing. He grabbed the handful of wild flowers that Susie had gathered and twisted them hard. Because they were so fresh they wouldn't tear at all.

He got even angrier when they wouldn't break. He rose quickly and threw the whole handful of them as hard as he could, back out toward the meadow. He threw hard with one leg up like a boy throws a baseball. The flowers fell in a scraggly shower as Susie watched.

Then he turned and shouted at her.

"Witch," he cried, "crazy, dumb witch!" Then he ran off across the meadow almost blindly as if he couldn't see where he was going.

Trevor

T HAT NIGHT Susie found it very hard to go to sleep. All night, pale shivery things stirred on the edge of her dreaming, startling her to wakefulness, thoughts of her own grandmother, and the boy on his haunches like that, rocking back and forth and talking about simples and his mother dying.

But going to school was the hardest of all. Susie had heard enough about what awful trouble kids got into when they were caught lying to their parents. What would Mrs. Farrell do? She could campus Lindy and make things really tough for her at home. She could make Lindy quit seeing Trevor and even stop her allowance. But whatever happened, she knew that Lindy was going to blame Susie for it, and Lindy was not very much on forgiveness.

But in all honesty Susie had to admit that even if she had known what was going on, there was no way that she could have brought herself to lie to Mrs. Farrell. What if Lindy's mother had asked Susie to call Lindy to the phone? She would just have to avoid Trevor and Lindy, that was all, try to keep out of their way until the whole thing blew over.

The entire day was a scary adventure. Susie thought of where Lindy would be and managed to be at another part of the building. She knew Lindy's schedule, so that part wasn't hard. But she wasn't sure about Trevor. She tried to keep an eye out for him.

It was after gym. Susie was hurrying up the stairs from her locker. There was just that little half-minute before the next bell, and the hallway was almost empty. When she turned at the angle of the stairs, Trevor was blocking her way.

He was grinning that ugly way he always did when he knew he was going to get to hurt somebody.

She turned and started down the stairs, but he was too quick for her. He caught both her wrists, spilling her notebooks and books in a clatter down the stairs.

"Hold it, blabber-face," he said in that hard low voice.

71

"You don't think you are going to get away with that trick, do you?"

His face was so close to hers that she could smell his breath hot against her, and tears came to her eyes.

"I got ways of handling troublemakers. I know how to keep your ugly mouth shut."

He was twisting her wrists so painfully that she wanted to scream. Then there was somebody at the top of the stairs calling. "Hey, Lammers, what's up?"

When Trevor glanced up, his hold on her arms looseened. But he shook her fiercely and threw her back hard against the railing. "I'm gonna get you, skinny. Just wait. I'm gonna get you GOOD."

By the time she got her books picked up, Susie was late for her last class. It didn't matter because she couldn't concentrate anyway. She felt sick at her stomach and terrified. There was no way for her to get away from Trevor if he really was after her.

She watched the hands of the school clock with a growing sense of dread. They raced through that hour as if an invisible force were pushing them. If she could only stay at school and not even try to get home.

She could call home. But how could she explain to Mother that she should bundle Mathew out of his nap and come and walk home with a seventh-grader?

When the bell rang, Susie thought she was going to be sick. Right there.

But the kids went out, and the teacher looked at her questioningly.

There was no point in waiting any longer; there would only be fewer people around if Trevor started something. She scooped up her books and got her sweater quickly, trying to lose herself among the crowd of kids who started off up Walnut Street. But at the corner of Magnolia most of them went straight. Susie, hearing her own feet clicking nervously, walked up Magnolia Street alone.

She was about a block from the station where Martin worked when Trevor appeared, leaping out from behind a hedge at her with a laugh.

"Gotcha," he yelled as if it were all a big game. A man who was watering his lawn straightened up with astonishment at the shout. Then he bent back to his work because he didn't understand.

Trevor had Susie by the arm and was twisting it. "Now you just walk, you little sneak," he said in a low voice. "I'm going to walk you to the corner, and then I'll beat the liver out of you. You'll never get Lindy in trouble again, I promise you that. Not Lindy, not anybody."

He was twisting her arm so hard that a great red welt started on her skin, and she began to cry.

"Let go," she wailed. "I didn't know. Lindy didn't tell me."

"Old innocence," he sneered. "Like you weren't just jealous."

Susie twisted in his grip. Across the street she saw Martin standing by the gas pump filling a car. He was staring at her and Trevor with a puzzled frown.

Trevor saw him looking and whispered in a low voice, "Don't you open your trap, skinny."

But at the sight of Martin's face she screamed. "Martin, Martin, help," she wailed.

Martin dropped the gas hose. Susie saw the fan of gas spreading on the concrete of the drive as Martin bolted across the street on his long, thin legs. But he was too late. Trevor twisted her by the arm so he stood facing her, then he hit her as hard as he could with his fist in her stomach, on her shoulder, and then on her face. She felt a sickening gush of blood flow from her nose. He threw her against the hedge just as Martin reached them. But Trevor was fast. He was across the hedge and through the lawn before Martin could catch him.

Martin stared after him only a moment, muttering something low and hard under his breath.

Then very gently he pulled Susie to her feet.

"My God, Runt," he said. "Come here."

The people from the gas station were frozen there watching, as Martin carried her towards them. Susie wished she could have curled up like a worm to hide. She was all stained and bloody, and her stomach was heaving as if she was going to be sick.

The woman from the car getting gas insisted on going to the rest room to help clean her up. The woman asked a million questions, but fortunately Susie didn't have to answer. The woman kept tripping one question right on top of another so Susie could just nod and hold her face up and try to stop her tears. Fortunately the woman's hands were as efficient as her tongue. After only a little while the blood stopped flowing, and the stains were only wet spots on the front of Susie's blue dress where the woman had rinsed them out.

Martin's boss at the station bought Susie a Coke and had her sit on a ledge by the flower bed in the sun and drink it while her dress got dry.

"Martin can take you home as soon as business eases up," he told her. "I hope I'm around to see it when that Lammers kid finally gets his comeuppance."

The Coke was settling to Susie's stomach. She ached all over, but at least her nose hadn't swelled up. It only felt sore, not bigger, when she touched it gingerly with her finger.

When Martin took her home, he stopped the car out front and stared at her a minute. "Look, Runt," he said quietly, "I don't want to go into this, but your folks have got about all they need to handle now. So if you could play this down?"

"You mean not tell them?" she asked, incredulous.

"Some day you'll understand," he promised her.

"Okay," Susie promised hesitantly. "But, gee, Martin."

He patted her hand. "That's a good sport," he said, winking.

Actually it would have been hard to tell her folks. For one thing her father was home, even though it was still early in the afternoon. Her dad's best friend John Burgess was there too, and they were talking in hushed tones with her mother in the front room. When Susie stopped at the door, her mother said brightly, "There are cookies in the kitchen, Susie," as if to suggest she should go right on in there and leave them alone.

Susie tried to eat the cookies, but they just wouldn't go down on all that Coke. She sat on the high stool waiting for Mr. Burgess to go away. Instead the voices rose and fell as if they could sit there and talk forever.

Susie hurt all over. Her arm ached where Trevor had twisted it, and along her back was a long bruised place where she had been thrown down.

She felt the voices moving farther and farther away. She was alone. There was nobody who even cared enough to notice how alone she was. The cupboard door swam before her eyes in a brimming of tears.

Suddenly she could stand it no more.

"I'm going out," she called into the living room without even looking at their faces. She heard a voice in reply, but she didn't stop to listen. As if they cared. As if they really cared.

She had never gone to the grove so fast before. She heard the dachshunds against the fence, but didn't even look. When she got to the grove, she sank on her gray stone with her head in her hands, waiting for the magic of the place to reach out to her.

Instead she heard the faintest-ever sound in the opening of the clearing. She knew it was the Clary boy before she even looked up. But he looked so different that something cold stirred in her chest.

He wasn't tearing things with his hand as usual. He only walked in quickly and sat on the rock across from her. He seemed paler, as if something had bleached the high color from his face. He stared at the ground between his feet for a long time.

"It's really rough up there now," he jerked his head towards the Clary house. "She's dying. She's really dying for sure. I heard the doctor telling my dad. She doesn't eat any more. Maybe a couple of bites but only to please my dad.

"I used to think about death coming, but it isn't like that. Death doesn't come. Life just goes. It just leaks away, and when it's gone there's only death left."

Susie felt a quick welling of tears behind her eyes and remembered Starchy. She tried to think of something to say, but she couldn't because of the hurt in her throat.

He lifted his eyes as if he was astonished. "And my dad is really sorry. You wouldn't believe that guy. He treats her like a special princess or something. Never leaves the room except to bring food or answer the phone. It's like he all the way forgot my mother and how mean they were to him. It's like he doesn't even *care* what I think.

" 'You understand or you don't,' " he quoted his father's words. Anger welled in his voice. "Well, I *don't* understand, that's what, and he can't make me, nor you nor anybody."

He was suddenly standing over her threatening her as he had that first day. Then he looked away. If he were a girl, she would have thought he was about to cry. Because she knew he wouldn't want her to see him like that, she looked down at the grass a long minute.

When he spoke again, his voice was strange, as if he were both confused and angry.

"Half the time she's all the way out of her head. Her voice changes and she laughs like a little kid. She talks about places she played and friends. She talks about my mother. She doesn't even remember how mean she treated her own child and all.

"It's like she's gone all the way back to being a crazy little girl. Like you," he said angrily to Susie.

Suddenly he reached in his pocket and pulled out a paperbound book. He threw it crossly at Susie's feet. "Here," he said angrily. "I brought you this. Simples for the simple."

Then he turned and left the grove swiftly, his legs

78

making a great brushing sound as he charged through the high, stiff grasses of the meadow.

When he was all the way gone, she picked up the book. It was a kind of journal. On the outside someone had written COUNTRY SIMPLES, *The Enchanted Herbs* in a fine, watery scrawl.

Susie turned the pages slowly, trying to read the wavering handwriting in the dying light. The book didn't seem to be in any sort of order. It was as if someone had started searching for plants, as Susie herself had done, and written them down just as she found them.

Beside some of the plant names there was a special raised mark. Some were marked, *"Healing,"* some were marked *"Food,"* and some were marked *"Magic."* There were wonderful names there too: Soloman's seal, and trillium, self-heal, and monkey flower.

Then she noticed that in between the names of the plants, the writer (it had to be old Mrs. Clary), had written other things. There was just a sentence at a time that had nothing to do with the plants—strange, puzzling thoughts that came in among the simples and stayed there like small dividers.

Holding the book carefully, Susie carried it home through the gathering dusk.

The End of
Everything

SUSIE ARRIVED home breathless with the boy's
book tightly under her arm. She opened the front
door quietly. Only Frump was in the living room, staring at her blandly with his great round eyes. At first she
was relieved that no one was about. From off in his
room, she could hear Mathew crooning to himself in his
crib. That meant that he had been fed and put down
for the night. The house smelled richly of spices and
meat, but there was a stillness, an emptiness that made
her pause inside the door.

"Mom?" she called, half-afraid of the quality of the silence in the house. "Dad?"

At her call, her father stepped from the kitchen. Susie was startled by the way he looked, framed against the light. He looked shorter, somehow, as if some awful weight had bent his shoulders, forcing him into the mold of an older, tireder man.

"We're in here, honey," he replied. In spite of his welcoming smile, she felt no reassurance. "Dinner's ready as soon as you are."

Susie glanced at the table, which was set for only three people. Her heart sank. They were going to have another of those tense meals with everyone trying very hard to ignore the fact that Carrie was walled off alone in anger behind the door of her room.

"Be right there," she replied, hearing the distinctive clatter that her mother always made when she started dishing up the food to serve.

She had only meant to put the boy's book in her own room and wash her hands. Instead, when she reached the hall, she stopped dead still.

The door to Carrie's room was not closed as it had been so much of the time these past weeks. Instead the door was all the way open, but Carrie was not there. Susie stared numbly at the room. It was neat, too neat. The disorder of Carrie's cosmetics was gone from the mirrored tray on the dresser top. The old stuffed Panda, that was always propped against the pillows, was gone.

Susie felt a sudden wild urge to go into the room and search for Carrie. It seemed to her that the very sense of Carrie was gone from the room, leaving it cold and desolate. Something hard and painful formed behind Susie's throat. She could hear voices in her mind, her mother's voice and Carrie's raised in anger at each other, her parents voices talking about the Clary girl who ran away and got married and died. Everybody fights with their parents sometimes, she told herself fiercely. That doesn't mean that the family has to go all to pieces. It can't. It can't.

She was still there in the hall when her father called again, softly so as not to disturb Mathew. "Come on, Susie," he urged. "The ribs are getting cold."

As she rinsed her hands and folded them in a towel, she stared at her reflection in the mirror. She must be all braced for what her parents would tell her about Carrie. What had Martin said . . . something about the folks having plenty on their minds and not to add anything? Had he known that Carrie was going to run away? She would have to be extra calm and grown-up so as not to make it worse for them than it already was. The very least she could do was take their news calmly.

She waited tensely as they all sat around the table. Then her father began to serve the barbequed spareribs just like always, lifting the meat, spooning ladles of rich red sauce thick with onions over it.

It was like a bad play where you knew what the lines were to be, but the inflection was false and amateurish.

"Potato, Susie?"

"Butter or sour cream?"

"Dig there in the bottom of the salad bowl. I put in some of those marinated mushrooms you like."

Susie stared at her father and then at her mother, at their closed, heavy faces. They weren't going to explain, she realized with astonishment. It was as if she were some stranger in off the streets that they must treat with extraordinary politeness.

"I am one of you," she wanted to yell. "Carrie is my sister." But instead, the hard place began to swell behind her throat. They had abandoned her as thoroughly as if they had run away themselves.

Her head throbbed and her whole body ached from Trevor's beating. The silence that had settled on the table was too much. When a bite of potato stuck in her throat and couldn't get past that hard lump, she put her fork down. She didn't mean for the fork to clatter in that noisy way. Her mother glanced up nervously.

"I miss Carrie," Susie said suddenly, looking directly at her father as if to dare him.

"We all do," he said calmly. "I've been sitting here trying to think of some way to tell you. Carrie will be away for a while."

"Visiting," her mother put in quickly, glancing at her husband as if for support.

For a minute there, Susie seized eagerly at the word. "Where?" she asked quickly. "Who is she visiting?" Susie thought of her grandmother back on the farm and of her Aunt Flo up in Eureka. Those were the only places that Carrie had ever gone visiting.

Before her mother answered, Susie saw her mother's eyes seek her father's face as if looking for an answer there. When she spoke, Susie realized with a cold sense of shock that her mother was lying to her.

"Friends," her mother said quickly, not meeting Susie's eyes. "She's visiting friends."

Susie waited for them to say something more, but instead they were busy with their food as if they had become hungry again just like that. She listened to Mathew's crooning from his room and watched Frump leap from the chair back and wave his tail imperiously as he passed towards his dish in the kitchen.

Not only was her mother lying, she told herself, but her father was backing her up. Maybe they weren't really *lying,* she told herself with quick guilt at the ugliness of that word, but at least they weren't telling her the whole truth. They weren't letting her be one of them like before. She shoved her napkin up by her plate all in a heap and went blindly through the house to her own room.

She was grateful that they didn't try to call her back because she barely made it inside her door before the tears came.

Susie lay a long time on her stomach on her bed trying to figure things out. But there were all sorts of loose ends that didn't fit together at all and yet would not come apart in her mind. Martin and Carrie had split up, that much was plain enough. Then Carrie had fought with Mom and Dad a lot . . . there was something in there about something that Carrie wasn't supposed to wear to school . . . and now Carrie was gone. The Clary girl was mixed up in it somehow, but in no way that Susie could figure out. Susie sat up suddenly and pressed her fists against her aching eyes. Surely Carrie hadn't run away like the boy's mother had done, to be married and die somewhere crying for home.

The very idea started Susie's tears again, and sometime in that crying she fell asleep.

When Susie finally stirred awake, it was all the way dark in her room. She turned on her bed lamp and piled all her pillows in a heap. On the top she put the Raggedy Ann pillow that Carrie had made her. Across the bottom in big embroidered letters it read, "I LOVE YOU." Nestled in the pillows she opened the book that the boy had given her and forced herself to read it all the way through to keep her mind away from Carrie's empty room.

Only at the very end did Susie realize that the private sentences, in between the comments and notations about the flowers, were like a journal. It wasn't like a diary that was kept every day. It was more as if Mrs. Clary had written a line or two and then waited, maybe years, before she chose to write again.

Susie read the book through again, skipping all the parts about flowers and only thinking about the sentences in between.

The first special entry was about a flower, but Susie counted it anyway because of what it said.

"I have come with the milkmaids," Mrs. Clary had written. "They are blooming along the edges of the fields. If milkmaids were really girls they would be gawky like I am. Too tall on the stem with that peppery nip to the root, as I have always been a prickly sort. I promise myself that I will *not* be as difficult a wife as I was a girl. I will never complain. Never."

After pages and pages of only flowers, the woman wrote again. "If my coming child is a girl, she will be named Angelica, for in the book this plant is called The Root of the Holy Ghost. This name will be a blessing on her."

It was strange to Susie that there was no mention of that child coming, nor any entries at all for a very long time except for the descriptions of flowers. Susie felt that many years had passed between that entry and the next which read, "After so many disappointments, I can barely contain my joy that Angelica has finally come. Today I transplanted a hawthorn into the grove as a symbol of hope for her."

After that were more small entries, like private whispers of a mother's pride.

"The young are gifted with magic," Mrs. Clary wrote. "Angie has made a magic place of the grove."

"The very birds of the sky know that Angie is of them."

"The towhee that Angie saved after his fall took wing today . . . and flew."

Then the personal sentences stopped again until very near the end of the book, when she wrote, "When I am silent in her grove, she comes to me. He will never let her come home to me again in any other way."

Susie noticed how Mrs. Clary's handwriting changed through the book. Near the end, the writing got smaller and tight together as if it hurt to form the letters. Close to the end she found the one that confused her the most. The letters were very badly formed so that Susie had trouble making the words out. When Susie finally did figure it out, she discovered that it was not a statement like the others but more like a question hanging there silent on the page.

"Where does my loyalty belong, to the needy or the beloved, to the old or the young, where the head sends it or the heart? I have watered her hawthorn with a lifetime of tears and still I do not know."

Susie wrapped the book carefully in some pink tissue paper she had saved from a Christmas box. Somehow she must get the book back to the boy and he must read it; not just look at the part about the flowers, but read the words that would explain his grandmother to him. Maybe like herself, he would be able to understand it even if he couldn't for his life explain it to anyone else.

That night Susie dreamed of the hawthorn as it had bloomed in the grove in early spring, masses of blossoms on small bare twigs and the small shrivelled apples of its last blooming still clinging to dry boughs.

Susie read herself to sleep with an old book she had had since the fourth grade. It was the only way she could think of to keep her mind from Carrie's being gone and from the dread she felt at meeting Trevor and Lindy at school the next day.

Even time seemed strange that next morning. It took Susie forever to get dressed and her arms felt weighted when she tried to eat her breakfast. She finally got it all down because her mother was watching, but she couldn't taste a thing.

Like things she had dreaded before, however, the day at school wasn't as bad as she had imagined it would be. Nor the next. Nor the next. She managed to avoid Lindy and Trevor. Though at home things were just as tense, she was even beginning to relax at school when she happened to notice, on Thursday, Trevor staring at her angrily across the hall. She turned away quickly so he wouldn't see the dark spot where he had hit her face, and she was afraid all over again.

And then Trevor was waiting to trap her when she came out of the cafeteria. He looked at her and laughed. "There she is," he said triumphantly. "The little sister. Big stuff aren't you? Better than anyone I guess. With your trampy sister running off to Berkeley with some old guy. You're the best, aren't you, winner-Spinner? But you wait. You just wait."

Susie, staring after him, saw Lindy waiting at the turn of the hall, Lindy who smiled up at him lovingly as they walked off together.

But it was Carrie that she thought about all afternoon. She knew exactly what she would do, who she would go to.

But the owner of the service station was manning the pump himself.

"Sorry, Susan," he said. "Martin's off today."

At her stricken look he added, "You might try ringing him at home. Need a dime?" He fished in his pocket.

Susie shook her head numbly and started on.

Then she glanced at the hill. She had the strangest feeling that the grove was calling her, that it needed her and that she must go. She hadn't been since Monday, she realized. It was almost like that first time, the way her feet went unerringly across the meadow without her paying any attention. The air was heavy with the fragrance of some hidden bloom and the hermit thrush was shouting "Pay!" from somewhere in the thicket. A faint blue curl of smoke rose from the Clary house like a small wavery genie released from a chimney.

Somehow she knew that the boy would be there before she even parted the branches to enter. But she hadn't expected to see him like he was.

He was sitting on her gray rock with his head on his knees. She stood a long moment before he noticed her. Even then he didn't look up. His voice was muffled from the way his head was buried in his arms.

"She's dead," he said flatly. "She's finally dead."

Susie stood awkwardly, waiting. She was trapped by the silence of those other meetings. She wanted to reach out to him, to lay a hand on his shoulder the way her mother did to her father when he was upset, but something held her back. She fought a quick rush of tears for an old woman she had never known. She stared at the hawthorn tree, at the small swelling rose hips where the blossoms had been, and waited.

"My father just sat there all that time and listened to her talk about Angie . . . that's what she called my mother. My grandmother wanted my mother to come. Or she wanted to come to my mom, but my grandad was old and sick and bitter. No one would have cared for him if she went. She chose wrong, you know that, don't you?" he raised his head angrily. "She should have come to my mom, not stayed with that cross old man."

Susie only stared at him. "The needy or the loved?" the old woman had asked. "The head or the heart?"

"My dad is just too much," the boy blurted suddenly. "He stayed there right to the end. And I never even told her I was sorry. I didn't *know* I was sorry until it was too late."

His head was on his knees again, and his shoulders moved with a slow rhythm like sobs. Susie leaned towards him. She would have touched him then, but a sudden sound from the opening to the clearing startled them both.

Trevor stood there, tall and broad and sneering.

"Thought you'd get away, didn't you? Thought I was blind or something, that I couldn't see you on that hill? But I didn't know you had a buddy." He sneered at the boy who had risen hastily, his face moist and bloated looking. "Don't much care who you sneak around with do you, fellow?"

Susie stepped back fearfully. But Trevor reached quickly and caught her arm. "Why don't you scream like before? Why don't you yell for help, you nasty little sneak? You don't think he'll help you do you, a bawl baby like that?"

The boy stared from Trevor to her. Susie wanted to scream but she couldn't. Her voice froze in her throat as Trevor laughed and struck her hard across the face.

It looked as if the fight would be over before it even began. The Clary boy stepped quickly between Susie and Trevor, breaking Trevor's hold on her arm.

"Lay off her," he said tersely, his voice still thick and funny from tears.

"Mind your own business, crybaby," Trevor said angrily, reaching for him.

Susie thought of Trevor's fights. He always won. He had always been able to beat anyone, because he was mean, meaner and bigger and stronger than the other fellows. But now he didn't seem to be half-trying. He only seemed anxious to get past the Clary boy to reach her. They wrestled hard, and the Clary boy caught Trevor in a funny hold twisting him back so that he couldn't get loose. Trevor cursed and writhed as Susie watched.

Then she saw the sudden glint of metal as Trevor wrestled his hand past his hip pocket. Her mind registered slowly, a knife. Trevor was pulling a knife on the boy.

"Look out," she screamed as the blade edged towards the Clary boy's thigh. "He's got a knife."

The boy froze. He loosened his hold on Trevor and

stared at her incredulously. In that moment Trevor broke free and brought the knife down quickly on the boy's leg. Susie watched with horror as a quick surge of scarlet stained the boy's trousers.

Only then did his eyes leave hers. He turned on Trevor like a wild animal. He seized Trevor's wrist, twisting until the knife dropped into the grass. Then he threw Trevor fiercely to the ground, pulling his arm back until Trevor finally grunted, "Enough, leggo."

The Clary boy pulled Trevor to his feet roughly, glaring at him.

"You want some more?"

"I'll go," Trevor answered, not meeting Susie's eyes.

"And lay off her from now on, okay?" The boy's tone was scary.

"Okay," Trevor grunted.

Susie stood silent as Trevor trailed off across the meadow. She didn't dare look straight at the boy. From the corner of her eyes she saw him swing his arms backwards as he watched Trevor go. Then he knelt and picked up the knife and threw it, as far as he could, across the meadow in the opposite direction. Then he turned to her.

She expected him to yell. She wouldn't have been surprised if he had hit her himself right there.

Instead he looked at her with a look of such complete disdain that Susie felt shriveled inside. Without a word he turned and walked off. He was limping from the cut on his leg, but he walked straight away with his back to her towards the trail of smoke that was all she could see of his dead grandmother's house.

Carrie

❧

SUSIE FELT as if her mind had left her body. She could watch herself walking down the hill and along the street to home, picking up Mathew for a toss and hanging up her school jacket, but she was no part of that Susie. The real Susie was only an aching hollow of betrayal. She was hated. She was really hated and despised, not as Trevor and Lindy hated her, but for a real reason. A numbness hung in her chest that was too big even for tears. "I will never be the same," she told herself miserably. "I can never *ever* be the same again."

Strangely, the household went on as usual. Her

mother called her to set the table and then they ate, Susie forcing every bite to go down past the hard numbness that lay beneath her throat.

While Susie did the dishes, she could hear her parents off in the living room discussing Mrs. Clary's death.

"I told John I would be a pallbearer," her father said. "In fact I was glad he asked me."

"Poor thing, she hadn't any friends," her mother replied.

"How could she?" Susie's father asked. "The children were barely reared before her husband took to his bed. I don't know how she took it all those years with that contentious old man. And apparently the kids are cut from the same cloth."

"Except Angelica," her mother reminded him.

"Except Angelica," he agreed quietly, "and that great Doug Born she married."

Because they were deep in conversation, they didn't pay any attention when the phone rang.

"Hey, Runt," Martin said. "The boss said you came by. Trouble?"

"I don't know, Martin," she hesitated. "Do you know where Carrie is?"

His voice sounded suddenly watchful. "Why do you ask?"

"My folks said she was visiting," she half-whispered, "but Trevor said something else."

"What?" he demanded curtly.

"That she's in Berkeley with some guy."

There was a long minute of silence.

"I honestly don't know," he said finally, then after a minute, "I got an idea, Runt. What if I pick you up after school tomorrow and we go check. Tell your folks I have to go to the East Bay to see something about college and asked you to come along. Tell them we'll have a hamburger or something. But don't mention Carrie."

"Want me to check now?"

"Yeah," he said. "I'll hold."

Her mother glanced up as Susie came in, her mind obviously still on the Clary family.

Susie repeated Martin's invitation carefully.

"Martin," her father said with surprise. "Why do you suppose he asked you?"

"We've always been friends," Susie reminded him. "And I think he's lonesome."

A fleeting unhappy look crossed her mother's face, and Susie knew she was thinking about Carrie.

"I don't see why she shouldn't go," Susie's mother said. "It would be a nice change, and it's not a school night."

"Just remind him that you need your beauty sleep," her father said, smiling at her.

"Don't get your hopes up too high," Martin warned Susie before he hung up.

Trevor was as good as his word to the Clary boy. He

avoided Susie as thoroughly as she had avoided him. By the time she got to the service station to meet Martin, Susie was too excited and scared about the trip to Berkeley to even worry about Trevor any more.

"How will we find her?" Susie asked as they started across the Richmond Bridge. A fleet of fishing boats hung at anchor beneath them, and a giant tanker was moving up the Bay, riding low in the water as if it were filled to the decks.

"I did a lot of asking around," Martin said. "I know where she is all right. What I don't know is whether she wants to see us."

When Martin slowed down and started searching for a place to park the car, Susie knew they were really getting close. An unexpected tightness came in her chest so that it was harder to breathe.

The after-work traffic on Telegraph Street was so heavy that Susie clung to Martin's hand as they crossed the street. His hand felt wet, the way hers got when she was scared, but when she looked up at him he smiled reassuringly.

Carrie was supposed to be in a sandwich shop. Susie figured that out as they went to the third place asking for her.

"I don't know much about all this," she confessed to Martin as they started off down the street again.

He shrugged. "There was a guy," he said shortly.

"She took a ring from him, and they were going to get married."

"But she's not grown-up," Susie protested.

"Grown-up is when you think you are," he said, not smiling at all.

"Does she love him?" Susie asked.

Martin looked at her. "I guess love is when you think it is, Runt," he said. "But then you can think again."

"You mean she didn't run away with him after all?"

"That's what I hear. It's more that she ran away from all of us—him and me *and* your folks, all of us."

It was dark before they found the right shop. Then Carrie wasn't there. Martin lied to the man, but Susie didn't stop him.

"I'm her brother," Martin said, "and this is her sister, Susie. We're only over for the evening and thought we'd look her up."

The man finished ringing up a sale before getting Carrie's address from the back. "You'd ought to catch her if she went straight home," he said. "She ain't been gone from here thirty minutes."

Martin drove slowly watching for numbers. He stopped at a tall thin house painted dark green. The lawn was neglected and something like an Indian bedspread was hung over one of the upstairs windows. He rang the doorbell for a long time, but nobody answered.

Susie waited in the car with her knees drawn up

against her chest. She couldn't imagine Carrie in that house or along this street. From the house next door she could hear a faint high wailing like someone practicing a flute, beginning and wavering and stopping to begin again.

Martin was turning from the front door in defeat when Susie saw the bus stop at the corner. Two or three people stepped down and started off quickly in the dusk. Then she saw Carrie.

Carrie didn't even look like herself. She walked along slowly with her shoulder bag banging against her side. Her hands were plunged deep into her pockets, and she was looking down as if she were studying the crosslines of the sidewalk.

Susie slipped from the car and walked towards her hesitantly. Carrie didn't even look up at her approach. Susie stopped and said softly, "Carrie?"

Susie watched Carrie's glance turn from disbelief to delight. Then Carrie's arms were tight around Susie and Carrie was crying. "Susie, Susie, baby. Why? How? ..." Then she stiffened and pulled herself back to stare at Susie, her eyes suddenly flat and angry.

"I miss you," Susie said, her voice wavering. "Martin and I."

Carrie looked past her to where Martin stood waiting, just standing there tall and waiting with nothing on his face at all, not even the edge of a smile.

Carrie's hand flew to her hair, pushing it almost automatically. She seemed to be trying to say something but couldn't.

"We missed you," Martin said. "Susie and I."

Suddenly Carrie's face crumpled. She flew at Martin and hugged him hard just like she had Susie. "Oh, me, too," she said. "Me, too." Susie heard Carrie's words disappear into tears, and she was crying there against Martin's jacket.

Martin nodded Susie towards the car, and Susie went, but she watched as Martin stood there a long minute, waiting for Carrie's crying to be over. Then they talked. A new moon rose reddish from the eucalyptus ridge on the hill, fading as it hitched itself higher in the sky.

Then Martin was slipping back into the car alone. Susie cried out, "Isn't she going to come home with us?"

Martin grinned and polished the steering wheel with the fat part of his hand there by the thumb.

"She says she doesn't want to be come after," he explained. "So we'll go get a sandwich now, okay?"

Susie sat silent while Martin ate two hamburgers and a large French fries and a whole chocolate shake. She didn't understand. She couldn't see what there was for him to be so happy about, humming while he gathered up sacks and napkins and tossed them into the litter basket.

Then strangely, he drove back towards that green house again.

They only got to the corner before Susie saw Carrie.

She was standing on the corner with a suitcase beside her. Her old stuffed Panda was strapped to it with a macrame belt. She had two hats on, one on top of the other like a circus clown. When they drew near, Carrie raised her thumb and cried, "Ride, mister?"

Martin whooped with laughter as he piled her things in the little jump seat in back.

"I want you to remember that I asked for a ride home," Carrie said to Susie after she was settled in.

"Okay," Susie said doubtfully, "but you're not allowed to hitchhike."

They laughed a lot more than her remark was funny, Susie thought, but it didn't matter.

Snatches and bits of their conversation passed over her as they crossed the bridge towards home.

"When I was tugged all those different ways," Carrie said, "I couldn't think straight. But once I got away—"

"Everything straight now?" Martin asked.

She nodded and leaned across the seat to kiss his cheek softly like she did Mother. "Everything straight," she said contentedly.

"Gosh, I hope you grow up smarter than your sister, Susie." She winked at Susie.

"And prettier too," Martin added, grinning sideways at Carrie.

That night should have been perfect. Susie's mother and father glowed with happiness once Carrie was home. They all chattered at once so loudly that they woke Mathew up who had to be brought out to be hugged and played with by Martin and Carrie.

Susie was full of the joy of the house again, the feeling that had come back into it with Carrie smiling and loving them all again. But then her father brought the pain tumbling back.

"I've asked Doug Born and his son for dinner here tomorrow night, Martin. I hope you and Carrie can join us."

"Oh," Carrie said, "that's the son-in-law that came home to take care of old Mrs. Clary. Sure, we'll be here."

It seemed natural to everyone that Susie was sleepy enough to pop off to bed early. Their laughter rose and fell beyond her closed door. But Susie sat in her dark room with the tissue wrapped *Book of Simples* in her hand, wanting to die before dinnertime the next day.

Facing Up

THE MOCKINGBIRD that had come with the
new year ran through his long recital of songs outside Susie's window as she cleaned her room. Susie
stacked her games and straightened the books and put
records back in their folders without even thinking
about them. From the other room she could hear
Carrie's voice rise and fall with telling, and through
it all her mother keeping Mathew on his schedule as
if he were a separate world that she ran with her
left hand.

Under the edge of her bed she found the Helen Keller book. It was overdue. Squatting there on the braided rug she read a little of it sort of out loud to herself so that her own words fell on her ears silently, making her remember and hurt.

It seemed so long ago that she had been sick and read the book and been led by her closed eyes across the open Clary meadow. So many things had gone wrong and been put to rights again. Carrie was back, happy and open with them again. Trevor was scared off, and she would somehow learn to live without Lindy. There was only the boy, a boy she never heard of until this spring. He would go away, and she could forget the way he looked at her with that look of sick betrayal. She could forget that, and everything would be all right again.

But she knew she was lying to herself. The deep hurt in his face was something painful she would have to live with forever. Still sitting on the floor, she took the Raggedy Ann pillow and hugged it tight, fighting back her tears.

Susie didn't hear Carrie coming until she was bending over her. Carrie smelled like a violet from a special soap she used, and Carrie's hand on her arm was cool and soft.

"What's the matter, baby?" Carrie asked, her voice secret near Susie's hair.

Susie shook her head. The tears squeezed through her lashes making a wetness on her cheeks.

"Can't I help?" Carrie asked, staying there, close and fragrant.

"Nobody can," Susie whispered hoarsely. "Nobody can at all."

Back before Mathew came when Carrie had babysat with her a lot, they had certain phrases they had used. Carrie went back to that time, asking the ritual questions gently.

"Is it an ouch?"

Susie nodded.

"An inside ouch or an outside ouch?"

"Inside," Susie said, snuffling in spite of herself.

In the old days Carrie had always prescribed a cookie or a rocking verse, but now Carrie caught Susie's hand and rose lightly, pulling Susie up.

"Dr. Spinner's cycling remedy," she announced. "We'll bike ride."

"I don't feel like it," Susie protested.

Carrie flattened the palm of her hand against Susie's cheek, wiping the tears away. "That's what doctors are for," she explained. "To make people feel well enough. Let's go."

It wasn't easy for Carrie to hold her bike back to wait for Susie. Carrie had a ten-speed that weighed even less than Mathew did. It liked to go like the wind with Carrie's hair flying loose. Susie pedaled like everything to keep up. Then Carrie stopped, braking at the fence that ran by the canal and grinning back at Susie.

They leaned over the fence and looked at the canal. The ducks had protested their coming, but almost immediately forgot about them in their bobbing search for food in the mud of the canal. Among the piping gulls overhead a single white egret cast a skinny reflection on the dark water. Off somewhere from one of the lagoon houses Susie could hear a dog barking excitedly, a small dog with a high-pitched, petulant voice.

"It's about those people that are coming tonight," Susie finally said into Carrie's waiting.

"The Clary son-in-law and his boy?" Carrie asked.

Susie nodded. "I did something really awful to him, that boy I mean."

Because there wasn't any sensible way to tell it, the different things all tumbled out sounding the same size and mixed up in their order. Susie heard herself telling about Lindy and Trevor and the funny absent way her parents had been and Helen Keller and the vow of silence. She was afraid that Carrie couldn't make head nor tails of it. Even the part about the boy sounded mystic and strange and not at all like it had been.

She knew for sure that she hadn't made sense when Carrie stood staring at the water for a long time, not saying anything at all.

"It's awful," Carrie finally said. "It's awful when you are growing up and things happen too fast. Things you don't really understand threaten you. I understand about Lindy. That part I understand too well." She turned to Susie. "Something sudden comes along all different and pressing, and it makes you giddy. You forget yourself, and you throw away big things for little ones just because the little ones are new. Lindy did that, and I feel bad about how sorry she'll be when she finds out what she's done."

Then she shook her head. "But that part about the spirit, and the vow. I know this sounds spooky but things like that, things that you do without understanding are very special. It's like your silence wasn't something you chose at all but something that boy needed so badly that something, maybe the spirit of that place, made you do it."

"You mean I couldn't have talked if I wanted to?" Susie asked.

Carrie looked almost embarrassed. "I said it was spooky."

"But now he's mad, mad as anything and he's coming tonight."

"He's only embarrassed," Carrie told her. "Inside he must know that you didn't set out to hurt him, any more than Lindy did you, or I did when I ran away to be by myself to get my head straight.

"But you have to tell him the truth. You can't lie to

yourself if you are telling someone else the truth. And facing up is hard."

Susie thought of the darkness of the Berkeley night and Carrie there on the curb with her panda bear and her thumb up. And Martin saying, "She doesn't want to be brought back. She wants to come on her own."

Susie was half-afraid of Carrie, always had been, she guessed. But she moved her hand awkwardly and tucked it inside of Carrie's arm.

"I missed you, Carrie," she said.

Carrie hugged her tight. Even without mascara Carrie's eyelashes looked thick and wet and curly.

"Let's go home and take that fat Mat off Mom's hands for a while. You'll do fine, just don't worry. You'll do fine."

Doug Born was tall and gray-haired and handsome in a way that Susie somehow didn't expect. His face was very thin with ridges running down the sides making his eyes look large. But his mouth had a quick smile as he bent slightly to touch Susie's hand.

"So this is Susie," he said happily, as if he had been waiting a long time to meet her.

She smiled at him with her heart thumping. Behind him, the boy from the wood was looking at her in that hostile way.

"My son, Derek," he said laying his hand on the boy's shoulder.

Susie only nodded at Derek while her mother did all those hostess things with chairs and offerings of cold drinks. Derek stood stock still, his legs a little far apart, daring her somehow.

Susie's father caught the awkwardness between them and turned to Derek, "Wouldn't you kids like to go outside while it's still nice? The Ping Pong stuff is there on the verandah."

When Susie turned to walk out, Derek followed, scuffing his feet. Susie felt a stillness in the room as if the grown-ups had suddenly been caught in the web of silence between the children. Then their voices began, all at once, the way grown-ups do when they have been surprised by a break in conversation.

Derek walked to the edge of the verandah where they were well beyond the view of the grown-ups. When she followed, he turned on her.

His anger was suddenly terrifying to Susie. Unconsciously her fists balled tightly against her face, which felt hot and tight against her hands.

"You must think you're something else," he said coldly. "Now the game's over you can laugh and laugh, can't you? Little smart-alecky, skinny kid making a total complete jackass out of a guy! I can just hear you now, telling your silly, giggly friends about it, about this guy you fooled," his voice cracked and broke.

"I never told anyone," she said very low.

He stood there staring at her.

"Not anyone?" he asked hesitantly.

"Not anyone at all," she said quietly.

"Your voice sounds lower than I thought it would if you had a voice," he said after a minute, then he flushed with anger. "Okay, just tell me what you thought you were doing, that's all. What was the whole bloody idea about?"

As she shook her head, the hair she had too hastily bound up fell down all around her neck. She clutched at it and twisted it back, tears suddenly hot under her eyelids.

"There wasn't any idea," she said. "It wasn't like that. That first day I was scared. I was scared something awful. I couldn't have talked to you or anybody. Maybe I thought if I didn't talk you'd go away and not come back."

"Not this sucker," he sneered at her. "I not only come back but I spill my whole guts out to you over and over again. What a dummy!"

"I never told anyone at all," she repeated. Then after a minute, "Later when I sometimes wanted to say something to you, I was afraid to. I—" she bit her lip, afraid all over, "I thought maybe it would help you to have somebody to just listen and care."

"Listen and care," he said slowly. Then he turned angrily and tore a sprig from the lemon tree and beat it against the tree again and again hard.

Susie watched the white blossom fall where he hit,

those small white blossoms tinged with lavender along the edge.

She bent over and picked the flowers up and held them in the palm of her hand in front of him. "Smell," she commanded him.

He looked at her, startled, and then bent over her hand. Then he realized.

"I'm sorry," he said. "Like that hawthorn in the grove."

She nodded.

"You really are a softie," he said after a minute. "You can't stand anything being hurt, can you?"

She shook her head.

"And you yelled when that guy pulled a knife on me," he reminded himself.

She nodded, not looking at him.

"We're going back to New York," he said suddenly. "My dad and I. We're going to sell that place, and I'll never come here again."

She looked at him, feeling empty inside her chest.

"I'll miss you," she said.

"Maybe I'll write," he said, swaggering a little. "Maybe I will, and then again maybe I won't. I'll see. I can beat you at Ping Pong."

"You really think so?" she challenged, offering him the choice between the red or blue paddle.

"I'm not sure at all," he decided out loud, grinning at her.

The evening went great after that. Dinner tasted delicious, and Mr. Born must have thought so too because he ate a lot. "Like a man who's been cooking for himself a long time," her father said after he left.

When Susie realized that the Borns were getting ready to leave, she excused herself and went into her room. She put the *Book of Simples* in a plain brown sack and folded it over a lot of times until it fit.

Her father glanced up curiously when she handed the wrapped book to Derek Born.

"It's a book we talked about," she tried to make her voice sound casual. "I thought it was great." Her father nodded absently and went back to his guest.

Derek was holding Frump, who lounged against his ear making such a huge purring sound that Susie could hear it a foot away. He shifted the cat's weight to take the book from her.

"Read it carefully," she told Derek softly. "Especially between the lines."

He stared at her, his brilliant blue eyes sharp on her face before he nodded his head only a little, like a pact.

The Wooden Swan

THOSE LAST FEW weeks before the end of school went very swiftly. Lots of afternoons Susie looked up at the Clary meadow and felt it calling her in that old secret way, but she never let herself go. She had said good-bye to Derek Born inside herself that last night at her house, and she was sure that he felt the same way.

Her science report on country simples had been a huge success with Mr. Laird. He asked her if he could keep it as a special exhibit, but Susie had her father make a copy of it in his office first. She needed at least a copy of it to remember by.

Her folks talked a lot about the Clary house. It had been put up for sale, but Doug Born wouldn't take offers from anyone who meant to develop the land around it. Finally when it sold to a retired professor from Stanford who wanted a country place to write books, everyone in town was glad.

There were ads all over for the sale of the Clary furniture, but Susie's mother didn't go. "Nothing from that big house would ever fit in here," she explained. "And I'm afraid I couldn't look at anything of Mrs. Clary's without thinking of the hard choices she had to make."

Before school was even all the way out, Susie's mother started shopping for her camp things because she was booked for the very first session. Then it was the last Saturday before camp, and Susie realized that she had to go back to the grove just one more time.

The rule was that you had to check into camp by two o'clock on Sunday. That meant that everything had to be packed the night before. As always they would leave midmorning with the back of the station wagon full of Susie's gear and Mathew's car seat between her and Carrie on the back seat.

Susie was glad that Carrie planned to go, too. Next to being pretty yourself, the next best thing was a sister like Carrie. It was always the same: the counsellors all flocked around and asked Carrie questions and brought her drinks of water in a dipper when she hadn't even said she was thirsty.

After that, for those first few days before they got everybody's name figured out, they always called her "Hey you, with the neat sister."

They would stop for lunch at the Nut Tree on the way up.

"Do you think that Mathew will be big enough to enjoy a ride on the little train?" her mother asked at dinner Saturday night.

"He'll like the Pied Piper anyway," her father said contentedly, cutting a generous square of lasagna for Susie's plate.

"And you're all ready, Chick?" her father asked.

"All except one thing."

"What's that?" her mother asked, her mind obviously on name tags and rainy weather gear.

"I just want to walk in the woods one more time."

"There's nothing *but* woods up there," her father laughed.

"I know," Susan replied.

That was the trouble. There was nothing but the woods up there. Never again could she be sure of the secret place and the blooming of simples, the red fox with his coal black whiskers framed in the darkening green. Nor Derek.

"You won't be late," her mother cautioned as she left.

The mockingbird ran through its whole course of songs, coming back again and again to the towhee probably because it was the easiest, Susie thought. But then she was past the mockingbird and the row of houses and into the wide field where the simples grew. The scent of summer lay on the grass, a dusty scent with no hint of rain.

The dark as always came first into the secret place. She closed her eyes a moment as she parted the leaves in order that the smell would be stronger, the heavy scent of held moisture, a little musty from the absence of sun.

She would sit on the gray rock and tell the grove good-bye with her eyes in the silence she had kept for Derek.

But the gray rock was hidden under Derek himself who glanced up when she entered, pressing a finger on his lips to caution her to silence. Then he looked down again to what was in his hands. It was a bird, but a funny one with only one wing carved. The other wing was only a rough chunk of wood against which he was moving his knife carefully.

"We're going to do it just like the other times," he said firmly. "You stay quiet and listen and I just talk to you. Okay? Just nod," he cautioned her quickly.

She nodded and sat down on the rock he used to use and watched his knife against the soft wood, moving gently but surely.

"I read my grandmother's book like you said," he told her. "Then I knew that this grove was a magic place for my mom when she was just a skinny kid like you. I decided that I could make you come with her magic. It didn't work right off, the first few times, but now you're here.

"I'm real good at carving," he told her. "I've carved a lot, mostly elephants through. Birds are harder because they stick out in little peaks that break off easy. Can you tell what kind of a bird this is?"

Susie shook her head.

"It's a swan," he explained. "My dad gave me the idea even though he doesn't know it. I told him all about you, after that night at your place. I told him how many times I talked to you while you only listened and nodded." His voice went a little funny. "And afterwards how you said you did it because you cared."

"My dad didn't say anything right off, he just pulled on his pipe making that funny sucking noise. Then he pulled a book off Grandma Clary's shelf. It was an old beat-up book, and it took him a while to find the right story in the index.

"Then he gave it to me to read. Have you ever read the story about the princess who had seven brothers turned into swans?"

Susie nodded, remembering only slowly.

"At the last you know she took this vow of silence to save them. They would have killed her for a witch except that the swans made it back in time. My dad said that story made him think of you."

Susie frowned, trying to figure it out.

"It wasn't the nettles that were the hard part, he told me, it was the silence. Keeping still when they called her a witch and a madwoman and when she knew that by opening her mouth she could have her own wish come true. But instead she listened.

"He said to me, 'What can you give a person in exchange for making a whole man out of a wild thing?' "

The boy finished the bird with the rough side of his knife, rubbing it a little so that the tip of the wing gleamed in the dying light.

"Even if I do elephants best, an elephant didn't seem right. So that's why this is a swan."

He thrust his arm out to her with the bird poised on his hand. A glint of light from between the trees struck it, making it glisten almost white.

She smiled and closed both her hands about it hard. It was warm in her hands, the way that only wood warmed by another hand can be. She had tears behind her eyes, but she must not let him see them.

When he stood up, he seemed taller than he had seemed when she saw him last. He seemed very grown-up there in the clearing, almost like a man.

"I am going to leave now and not look back. That way I won't mess up what I like to remember best. Right?"

She nodded.

"Wait a minute," he said in that bossy way. "You get over on your own rock the way you were and look that way like you did the first time. Too bad you don't have those funny clothes on, like before."

She grinned. How was he to know that those jeans were uncomfortably tight from the "filling out" she had done since she had been sick, and that just lately she had begun to stick out in front enough that she wouldn't be caught dead in that tight old T-shirt.

She didn't watch him go because she knew he wouldn't want her to see him in case he looked back.

She sat there a long time, turning the carved swan in her hand. As the darkness filled the grove up all the way, she could feel the grove accepting her as a part of it.

She did not need the mothlike sweep of the owl through the darkened air nor the scent of the fox to reassure her. The friendly silent darkness knew no time; all who had been here were a part of it as were all who might one day come.

But had she ever been able to name the spirit of that grove? The question troubled her all the way home. She could make up a name, a wild fanciful name that no one else would even understand if she wrote it down. But that wouldn't be right. The spirit of the grove had its own name and some day it would come to her, just like that.

She would wait.